A
Lancaster County
Christmas

Books by Suzanne Woods Fisher

Amish Peace: Simple Wisdom for a Complicated World
Amish Proverbs: Words of Wisdom from the Simple Life
Amish Values for Your Family: What We Can Learn from the Simple Life

A Lancaster County Christmas

Suzanne Woods Fisher

Revell

a division of Baker Publishing Group
Grand Rapids, Michigan

© 2011 by Suzanne Woods Fisher

Published by Revell
a division of Baker Publishing Group
P.O. Box 6287, Grand Rapids, MI 49516-6287

Printed in the United States of America

ISBN 978-1-61793-296-0

Scripture used in this book, whether quoted or paraphrased by the characters, is taken from the King James Version of the Bible.

This book is a work of fiction. Names, characters, places, and incidents are the product of the author's imagination or are used fictitiously. Any resemblance to actual events, locales, or persons, living or dead, is coincidental.

Published in association with Joyce Hart of the Hartline Literary Agency, LLC.

To a very special woman,
a friend extraordinaire for nearly thirty years,
Nyna Dolby.

Two Days before Christmas

The first thin flakes of snow had begun to swirl. Mattie Riehl glanced out the buggy windshield and up at the troubling clouds during the trip into town for a doctor's appointment. When they reached the parking lot, she hesitated before climbing out of the buggy. "The sky is more ferocious looking than when we left home."

Solomon, her husband, reached his hands around her waist to help her down. "We'll be home in plenty of time before it hits."

"Bet we'll get fresh snow for Christmas!" Danny nosedived over the front bench of the buggy and slipped out behind his mother. He lifted his small face to the sky, scanning it for snowflakes.

"Looks like we might," Mattie said. She straightened her son's glasses and turned to her husband. "I still don't think this appointment is necessary."

Sol paid her no mind. "Well, we're already here. The doctor thought it would be wise, Mattie. Just to be safe."

When she lifted her head, her eyes caught her husband's gaze. A look of joy and suffering, woven together. *That's what these last few weeks have been like. Love and pain, joy and suffering.* Sol bent down and tugged the felt brim hat on his son's forehead, then gently steered Mattie into the doctor's office.

Mattie and Danny sat down in the empty waiting room while Sol spoke to the receptionist. Mattie glanced around the room, amused. It was covered with English-style Christmas decorations. Gold garland draped the walls, Christmas cards were thumbtacked onto a bulging bulletin board, an artificial spruce tree sat in the corner, blinking its colored lights. The door opened and a young English girl swept in, nearly knocking down the wreath made of shiny gold and silver metal sleigh bells that practically engulfed the door. The girl steadied the wreath before she walked up to the desk to check in.

After Sol finished talking to the receptionist, he sat down next to Mattie. "It'll be a few minutes. The doctor's running behind."

Danny walked around the room, examining the walls. "Dad, where is that music coming from?"

Sol pointed out the speakers in the ceiling. Mattie hadn't even noticed the music until Danny mentioned it. Then she heard strange lyrics pour out: "Grandma Got Run Over by a Reindeer." She and Sol exchanged a startled look.

"Englische Schpieles," Sol murmured and shrugged his shoulders. *English music.*

The English girl, still talking to the receptionist, pulled off her hat and scarf. Hair the color of ripened peaches spilled around her shoulders.

"Is that a Burberry scarf?" the receptionist asked the girl.

"What kind of a berry is a burr-berry?" Danny asked Mattie, but she hushed him before he could ask another question.

Once her son got going, nothing stopped him. He had more questions than there were answers.

Mattie overheard the English girl ask the receptionist if she could just pick something up and go.

"No, no," the receptionist said. "The doctor always likes to talk to his patients before he renews a prescription."

"Why?" the girl asked, her voice a little louder, exasperated. "I just saw him six months ago."

The telephone rang and the receptionist turned her attention to it, grabbing the receiver as she pointed to a chair for the girl to sit in. "Take a seat," she mouthed. "He'll be with you as soon as he can." She pointed to a basket of candy canes. "Help yourself."

The girl picked out a candy cane, turned slowly around, and found an empty seat.

Mattie had it wrong. The English girl wasn't a girl at all, but a woman. A woman with a very odd haircut. It was longer on one side than the other. Peculiar! Other than the cockeyed haircut, the woman was quite lovely, Mattie realized, with blue eyes that tilted at the corners and a soft, round face. But there was turmoil behind those eyes—as if the world were all at sea. Danny whispered a question to Sol and the woman startled, as if she had forgotten anyone else was in the room. She looked curiously at Mattie and Sol and Danny as she took in their Plain clothes—a look of puzzlement Mattie was long accustomed to. Then Danny left his father's side to cross the room to the English woman. Mattie reached out to stop him, but Sol put a hand on her knee. Danny was known for wandering off, talking to strangers. Sol always said to let him be, that it was in his nature to be curious. Mattie used to be more agreeable, allowing Danny room to be adventurous, but over the last year or so, she could feel herself changing in a way she didn't like and couldn't help.

Danny sat down next to the woman and showed her a wooden whistle. The woman looked at the whistle politely, but seemed a little uncomfortable around a child, especially a Plain one. Danny didn't seem to notice her discomfort, but then, that was Danny. He assumed everyone liked to talk to him. "My dad made this for me. For my birthday." He looked up at her. "Want to hear what it sounds like? It's an owl whistle."

"Danny," Sol said in a warning voice. "You're in a doctor's office."

As soon as Danny mentioned the word "owl," the English woman visibly relaxed. "He won't bother anyone," she said, her eyes glued to Danny's whistle. "It's just us in the waiting room. I'd like to hear it."

Danny's cheeks puffed with air as he blew out three short hoots. "It's a screech owl. Everybody thinks a screech owl should sound screechy, but it's really a hoot sound. It's the barn owl that sounds so screechy." He then imitated the ear-piercing sound of a barn owl. "I found a baby barn owl with a broken wing. I feed it mice every day."

The woman fingered the wooden whistle. "Must be nice to have an owl for a pet."

"Oh, it's not a pet," Danny said solemnly. "Wild animals should never be pets. My dad helped me set the wing, and after it's healed, we're going to release it."

"I've always admired owls," she said. "I think I read somewhere that owls are the only birds that fly without making any sound."

"That's true!" Danny said. "And they're not waterproof like other birds. They get soaking wet and weighed down by their soggy feathers so that they can't fly. If an owl can't dry off quickly, it can shiver with cold and die." He wrapped his arms around himself and started to shake, to show her how a wet, cold owl acted.

The woman burst out with a laugh. "How old are you?"

"Six-and-a-half," Danny said, as if it were one word. He poked his spectacles higher up on his nose. "How old are you?"

"Danny!" Mattie said sharply.

A slow smile softened the woman's features. "It's only fair. I asked him. He's asking me." She turned to Danny. "I'm twenty-five. And my name is Jaime. Jaime Fitzpatrick." She held out her hand to Danny.

He reached over and shook her hand. "Danny Riehl."

"Are birds your favorite animals?" she asked.

He wrinkled his nose, a sign he was deep in thought. "I haven't decided yet."

"I used to take pictures of rare birds," Jaime said to Danny. "And once I photographed the migration flyway during the Audubon Christmas Count."

"I know about that!" Danny said. "My cousin lives in Ohio and rides bicycles to count the birds. My cousin and his friends set records on how many birds they counted." He sat down next to her. "What do you take pictures of now?"

Jaime hesitated. "I take pictures of people, mostly. I've been working at Sears Portrait Studio. Just down the street from here."

"You don't take pictures of birds anymore?"

"Not like I used to. But it's my favorite thing—to take pictures of nature and wildlife. It's not easy to do. Movement is a photographer's greatest challenge, and birds are always on the move. But then you've got a trade-off—because natural light is so much better than artificial lighting."

Danny's face scrunched up. "If you like to be outside so much, then why would you work inside?"

A strange expression crossed Jaime's face. "Well, the backdrops for the portraits can make it look like a person is outside." She glanced at her watch.

"Danny, du hast genug sach Fraugt," Mattie said. *Danny, you've asked enough questions.*

The nurse opened the door and asked sternly, "Did somebody let a wild bird loose in the waiting room?" Her face broke into a mischievous grin as Danny's eyes went round. "Why, lo and behold, it's not a wild bird at all. It's just a wild *boy*!" She winked at Danny and he giggled. "We're ready for you now, Mrs. Riehl." She turned to Sol. "Shouldn't be a long appointment."

"Danny and I will go outside," Sol told Mattie, giving her a look of reassurance.

"We can play catch with snowballs!" Danny said.

He ran to the door and opened it, letting in a blast of cold air. Then he turned and waved goodbye to the English woman. She tossed him the candy cane and he caught it in his mittened hands. He turned to Mattie, a silent request to eat it. She nodded, and he gave the English woman what Sol called his jack-o'-lantern grin. Four front teeth were missing.

As soon as the Amish woman disappeared into an exam room, the nurse returned to the waiting room and motioned to Jaime to follow her into the doctor's office and step on the scale. She moved the weight until it finally balanced, whistling two notes: up, down. "You're sure inching your way up that scale!"

Jaime studied her feet. "Must be these shoes." Along with her new hobby of grief snacking.

"I don't think so, hon."

Jaime frowned at her, but the nurse was oblivious as she scribbled down the weight. "Five pounds is really not all *that* much."

The nurse snorted. "No, but ten sure is, sugar."

Jaime winced. The funk she'd been in since her mother's death last summer was taking its toll in more ways than just increasingly uncomfortable clothes.

As the nurse wrapped the blood pressure cuff around Jaime's arm, she turned to face the instrument on the wall. Long blond hair swung around the perfect oval of the nurse's face. Jaime poked an errant curl behind her ear and wondered how the nurse's hair fell like that—sleek and smooth—unlike her own hair, which continued to defy the new straightening product she'd paid way too much for.

"Born that way," she said, reading Jaime's mind.

"I figured," Jaime sighed. Her own hair was the curse of her existence, especially on a windy winter day when even industrial-strength styling gel couldn't keep her hair settled down.

The nurse rolled up the cuff and stuffed it into the holder on the wall. "Your hair is . . . unusual."

Okay. Now the nurse had sailed past mildly irritating and was flirting in the annoying zone.

"You don't see that color every day . . . unless it's out of a bottle."

This nurse had a knack for poking Jaime's raw spots: her blossoming weight, her unruly hair. What was next, her ever-so-absent father? Or better still, what about her fragile marriage? "Well, it's not," Jaime said, sounding a tad more defensive than she intended. At least her hair color added some flash to the rest of what she considered her very ordinary features. She'd always liked her eyes, though, and she liked to believe their slight tilt gave her a mysterious look. As a child she used to wear a scarf over the bottom half of her face as a veil and pretend she was a Moroccan spy.

"So, doll, are you ready for Christmas?"

Jaime never understood why people used diminutives in place of names. Hon, doll, sugar. Why didn't the nurse just admit she couldn't remember Jaime's name? "This year will be a little different. We're not really celebrating. We're going away for Christmas."

The nurse turned to leave. "Christmas has a way of coming, wherever you might be." She snapped Jaime's chart shut. "Dr. Engel will be seeing you today. He's on-call for the regular doctor."

Jaime's head snapped up. "What happened to Dr. Cramer?"

"Dr. Cramer is at his daughter's preschool recital. Dr. Engel agreed to take over his office visits today, as a favor." She tilted her head. "Dr. Engel will just be a moment. Or two."

The nurse hummed along with the tinny music piped in through the ceiling speaker: "I Saw Mommy Kissing Santa Claus." She smiled distractedly at Jaime as she reached for the door. The door was decorated as a giant gift—covered with shiny foil wrapping paper and taped with a big red bow. The bow came loose and fluttered to the floor. "Blasted bow," she muttered as she picked it up and pressed the sticky side against the door. "These decorations have been up since before Thanksgiving. I'll be glad when Christmas is over and this place can go back to looking like a doctor's office."

As the door closed behind the nurse, Jaime glanced at her

wristwatch and weighed her options. She was frustrated with herself for leaving this errand to the last minute. She heard a gust of wind blow a tree limb against the building and walked over to the window to look at the ominous clouds.

She saw two black hats outside—the Amish father and his son gathering snow that had dusted the ground, packing it into balls, and pelting each other. The Amish boy's snowballs weren't packed hard enough and they splayed apart after release. Soon there was as much snow being flung through the air as rested on the ground. The sight made her laugh out loud. That little boy was so cute! Strawberry blond hair, thick blond lashes framing saucer-sized brown eyes, and freckles across his nose, like someone had sprinkled it with cinnamon. The nosepiece of his eyeglasses was wrapped with adhesive tape. And such round cheeks! He didn't walk so much as he bounced; he didn't talk so much as he bubbled over like a shaken-up can of soda. She wasn't really one to notice children. C.J., her husband, was the one who noticed kids, in restaurants or at parks. But then, he was a teacher.

The little boy nailed his father square in the face with a snowball. Jaime's gaze shifted to the father. She felt a pang of worry for the boy, fully expecting the father to start bellowing. Instead, she saw the father wipe snow dramatically off his face and laugh. Then he chased his son and grabbed him in a bear hug. That sight . . . it was so unexpected, so charming, she framed it in her mind like a photograph. If her mother were still here, she would've turned it into a Currier & Ives type of Christmas card, with such a caption as "The best things to give your children aren't things!"

Tears pricked Jaime's eyes. She had to stop doing that. Stop cobbling together imaginary conversations with her mother as if she were still alive. She wasn't.

Jaime's mother had worked as a writer for an inspirational greeting card company. She spent all day thinking up verses and phrases: An Easter card that read, "No bunny loves you like Jesus!" Or a pick-me-up card: "Exercise daily! Walk with Jesus!" These platitudes—always with exclamation points!—infused her mother's everyday speech in a way that used to embarrass Jaime, especially around her friends.

No longer.

She leaned her forehead against the cold windowpane. A moment ago she had been laughing. Now she felt an aching sadness that she couldn't understand.

Jaime heard the slightly accented voice of the Amish woman talking to the nurse as she walked down the hall to leave.

Then the door to the examining room where Jaime was waiting opened slowly. The doctor shuffled in and gave her a warm smile. He had penetrating blue eyes and a shock of white hair. But he was old, so old that Jaime's heart sank. *This won't be quick.* Jaime extended her hand to shake his. "Dr. Engel, I'm Jaime Fitzpatrick. And I won't take but a moment of your time."

The doctor reached out and clasped her hands with both of his as if he were greeting a long-lost friend. Or maybe it was the way he looked at her straight on, in a manner that was so frank and plain it might have been mistaken for rudeness if his blue eyes had not been so kind.

"Nonsense! I've got all the time in the world." Dr. Engel pulled up a chair and eased himself into it, facing Jaime. "So, Jaime Fitzpatrick. How are you today?"

Something in his greeting, his solicitous tone as he asked how she was feeling, made a sick anticipation rise from the center of her stomach. It felt as if time was slipping into slow motion, matching Dr. Engel's leisurely pace. Even the song now playing on the radio was an instrumental version of "Silent Night."

Jaime lowered herself to her chair. "I really just stopped by to get a prescription refilled. Dr. Cramer prescribed it for me awhile ago." She enunciated each word carefully in case he was possibly deaf on top of being slow.

Dr. Engel opened Jaime's chart, scanned it, humming as he read, then let it drop on his lap. He leaned back in his chair. "You didn't answer my question. How are you today?"

"Fine. I'm just fine." *Hurry, hurry, hurry!*

"A note here said that Dr. Cramer suggested getting some counseling along with the sleeping pills. Have you done that?"

Jaime folded her hands in her lap. "No. I've solved my problem."

"Is that right?" Dr. Engel lifted his bushy eyebrows and tapped the chart. "So that's why you're here today, because you're sleeping so well?"

She sighed and tucked a loose curl behind her ear. "Not exactly 'well,' but . . ." *Not exactly at all.* "Look, I don't use the pills every night. Just when I really need them. I've had a lot on my mind and I've needed a clear head to make good decisions."

Dr. Engel picked up her chart, peering at it through his bifocals. "So your mother passed away recently?"

Jaime shifted in her seat and crossed one leg over the other. "Last summer."

"So this will be your first Christmas without her."

She stiffened. *Oh pull-eez.* Did he think she wasn't aware of that?

"Grief takes awhile to work through. It can't be rushed."

"I'm fine. Really." She froze when she noticed that Dr.

Engel's gaze was on her foot, wiggling back and forth in the air.

"I know I'm old school, but I believe that pain can be the most important tool in a person's life. It forces a person to pay attention to something that needs to be changed. I worry that drugs like sleeping pills mask pain just enough that the real root of the problem gets buried, deeper and deeper. A problem—even something like grief—just doesn't go away until it's dealt with."

Jaime glanced out the window and saw large snowflakes, drifting in the wind. "I'm making a change. A big one." Starting today. One hour ago, to be exact, when she told her manager at Sears Portrait Studio she was quitting.

"Change isn't the same thing as addressing grief, Jaime. It'll just keep resurfacing. Avoidance is not a way to cope. There are better coping methods."

"Such as?" Jaime said coldly. She didn't mean to sound so rude. Why was she acting so prickly with everyone? She always had a tendency to speak before thinking, but today, it seemed as if she had no filter at all.

This doctor meant well, she had no doubt, but he had no right to be poking into her private business. Dr. Cramer never asked these kinds of probing questions. But she needed those pills! This morning, while photographing a fussy elderly woman and her cat, she felt a wave of dizziness from lack of sleep. Her entire body ached with fatigue. She simply could not get a good night's rest. She would lie in bed and watch the glowing digital numbers on the alarm clock flip over and over, her mind bubbling with anxieties.

"Some folks find solace and guidance in faith, for one."

Oh no! Talking about religion was like walking toward a bee swarm, just waiting to get stung. Same thing. She was determined to avoid *that* particular topic and all the unsolvable turmoil that came with it. Jaime rose to her feet. "I really need to be on my way. If you wouldn't mind giving me the prescription slip, I'd like to get going before the storm hits."

Dr. Engel held her eyes for a long moment. Then he handed her the writ. "Dr. Cramer had already filled it out for you when you called in this morning." He eased himself to a stand, creaking as he went. "Jaime, you just have to ask for help when you need it."

Isn't that why I'm here? Jaime gave him a stiff smile, took the writ, and stuffed it—along with his surfeit of advice—in her purse.

The snow was falling steadily, damp and clinging. The wind had whipped up, finding every crack and crevice in the buggy to slip through. At moments like these, Sol thought back to that time in his life when he was in his Rumspringa and hid a car from his folks. He didn't object to living the Plain life, but on bitter winter days he did think back fondly to that car. He could blast on the heat, roll up the windows, cut off the wind, and crank up the radio.

He glanced over at Mattie as she spread the buggy blanket over her lap. What would she think of his thoughts? She was so pure, his Mattie. He doubted she ever had a taste for the worldly life, not like he did. Not like Zach did. Mattie's seventeen-year-old cousin had been living with them since summer. Zach ran with a wild group of friends, a choice that had caused growing tension between him and his parents. All spring, his parents were at their wits' end. Finally, after one major mishap, his father had given him an ultimatum:

get baptized or get out. So Zach got out. With no place to go and no money in his pocket, Mattie scooped him up like a stray puppy and insisted he live with them. It wasn't that Sol was entirely unsympathetic to Zach's plight—he was no stranger to teenage shenanigans. When he was not much older than Zach, he had gone so far as to leave the community and abandon the girl he adored because he had a once-in-a-lifetime opportunity to pitch for the Lancaster Barnstormers. It was a wonderful, awful time. He knew firsthand the dangers and temptations of the outside world. He knew the pain and heartache he had inflicted on those he loved.

When Mattie told Sol she wanted Zach to stay with them, he thought it over and finally agreed. Sol hoped he could help Zach avoid the regrets he had—but it was starting to trouble him to see the influence he had on their Danny. Danny adored Zach. To him, Zach was the older brother he never had. He talked like him, he walked like him. He was even starting to wait to dress in the morning until he saw what color shirt Zach was wearing. It shamed Sol to admit this, but he felt as if Zach had displaced him in his own son's life. Danny used to imitate Sol the way he was imitating Zach.

And behind it was the nagging worry that Zach was bringing the outside world into their home.

Sol could already see Danny would have a difficult time of it when he reached Rumspringa. Danny's mind was eager for new things, new information. Could the Plain life satisfy a mind like that? So much of their life was routine. There was great comfort in routine, he knew, and he had grown to love his life. But he understood the longing a young man might have for the excitement of the world.

Mattie shivered and snuggled closer to him.

"So what did the doctor say?"

She kept her gaze on the swishing tail of the horse. "He said not to lose hope. Miracles can happen, he said." Mattie's voice was sweet but thin. She spoke with forced cheer, like those narcissus bulbs she put in little paper cups every January and lined up on the kitchen windowsill.

"That's exactly right," he said reassuringly. His spirits lightened slightly. He put his arm around her and drew her close. She was still weak from her miscarriage, just four weeks ago. "I don't think we should be giving up, Mattie," he whispered. "You always said we should expect miracles in this life."

"The Lord God had already given us a miracle," she said quietly. "Danny is our miracle."

Hearing his name, Danny popped up and hung over the backseat of the buggy. Mattie tapped the tip of his nose.

"He is indeed," Sol said, "but that doesn't mean the Lord won't grant us another miracle."

They had such high hopes for this pregnancy. Mattie hadn't conceived since Danny was born, and then one day this fall, she told Sol she was going to have a child. Their prayers had been answered! Until the day after Thanksgiving, when the bleeding and cramping started. And their hope was extinguished.

Mattie tucked her arm through Sol's and leaned her chin on his shoulder. He turned the horse into the driveway that led to their farmhouse. The horse picked up his pace, knowing that a hay dinner and a warm stall would be waiting for him. Sol pulled the buggy as close to the kitchen door as he could and helped Mattie inside, hoping she might lie down for a few minutes before dinner. He sent Danny directly to the barn to help Zach feed the animals. He unhooked the horse from the buggy traces, led it inside the barn to its stall, and pushed the buggy into the barn to keep it sheltered. Snow crunched under his feet as he crossed the yard to the house.

In the kitchen, Sol pushed the coals around in the woodstove and added logs to warm up the downstairs. Mattie was checking on Buster, Danny's baby barn owl. Mattie babied Buster and kept it in the kitchen, even though Sol assured her the owl would be fine in the barn. Mattie didn't agree. So Buster stayed in a cozy box by the stove.

He smiled as he watched her crouch by the box, talking softly to Buster. Then his smile faded. He knew she had given up hope for another baby. He could see it in her eyes, even the way she nurtured that silly barn owl.

Mattie hadn't just lost her hope. She had lost her joy.

Jaime stood by the front door of the doctor's office and put on her hat and scarf, bracing herself for a shock of cold. She buttoned her top coat button. It looked bitter outside, with dark clouds racing across the sky. Just as she stuffed one hand into a glove, Dr. Engel opened the waiting room door and called her name.

"Would you mind doing me a favor? That Amish boy left his toy. They live on a farm right on the edge of town . . . not far from the highway."

She hesitated. The snow was sticking to the road, and she was anxious to get to the drugstore to pick up her prescription before her husband expected her at his school. She didn't want C.J. to know she had been to the doctor. He worried she might become dependent on sleeping pills. "Maybe they can just come back and get it."

The nurse with the perfect hair popped her head out of

the reception window. "That Amish mama miscarried just a few weeks ago. She's been trying and trying to have a baby." She clucked her tongue.

Oh. The extra ten pounds that had crept up on Jaime's small-boned frame since her mother's death no longer seemed like such a big problem.

Dr. Engel gave the nurse a look, and she quietly closed the window. He walked up to Jaime. "After today, I won't be seeing the Amish woman for a while. She's going to be just fine." He put the whistle into her gloveless hand and curled her fingers around it. "Amish kids don't have a lot of toys. This one must have been pretty special for him if he brought it into town."

"Not so special that he couldn't have remembered it," Jaime said.

"Boys are boys. And no boy should be parted with his whistle. You don't mind, do you?"

Do I really have a choice? "Fine. I'll take it."

Dr. Engel gave her vague directions about how to reach the farmhouse. "When you see an old roadside cemetery—with small plain markers behind low stone walls—then you're getting close. Turn left into the driveway when you see a long white fence that wraps along the road. The Riehl farm is hard to miss—big unpainted barn. Green shutters. White clapboard. Big wraparound porch out front." He held the door open for her. "Not to worry. You'll know it when you see it."

Jaime ran to her car and turned on the ignition, setting the heat to full blast. She sat there for a while, waiting for the car's engine to warm up. It was a habit ingrained by her husband. C.J. was deliberate about taking good care of cars—changing the oil regularly, getting tune-ups, giving the engine time to get warm. He was deliberate about everything.

As she waited, she looked more closely at the whistle. There was something about the way that Dr. Engel asked her to deliver it—the way he looked at her—that made her think this whistle had some kind of special significance.

Though she'd lived in Lancaster County all of her life, she had never really known any Amish. Other than a brief chat here and there at an Amish roadside fruit stand, today's conversation with the little boy was the longest one she'd ever had with an Amish person. It seemed there was an invisible wall between the two cultures. They felt it. She felt it.

She held the whistle up to her lips and blew on it, gently at first, then louder. The funny squeaks made her laugh out loud. It felt good, easing the tight feeling in her chest that had been her constant companion lately.

She turned on the wipers to knock some snow off the windshield. The entire parking lot was covered with a thick, one-inch layer of snow, just in the time she had been in the doctor's office. She listened to the weather report on the radio and cringed when she heard the weatherman warn people to prepare for power outages and get supplies to last for a few days. She and C.J. absolutely, positively had to get to her father's tonight. Her father had told her he had a huge surprise waiting for her, and she had a pretty good idea what it was going to be.

Mattie covered the casserole with tinfoil and slipped it into the oven. The air was redolent with Danny's favorite meal: roast pork and oven potatoes. Danny would be happy when he caught a whiff of this, she thought. She made a double portion so that there would be plenty for tomorrow's lunch. She really should start cooking in smaller batches, but she just didn't seem to be able to. A casserole as big as the one she just made would have filled up four of her six brothers. The bulk of her mother's time, like most every woman, was spent preparing meals. Not so for Mattie. She should be finding the good in that, she knew, but instead she looked at the big kitchen table and thought about the children she had hoped would fill it. She took out forks, knives, and spoons and set four places at the table—the pine harvest table that Sol had built for her when they were newly married.

Dear Sol. He was trying so hard to make things a little better. How she loved him—his steadiness, his honesty, his humor, and his kind, kind heart. The buggy ride home from the doctor's office today nearly undid her. Sol's eyes, so sad, searching her face, trying to see into her heart, hoping there would be good news. He liked problems he could fell like trees, problems he could solve. Mattie's barrenness left him confounded.

She ran a hand along the tablecloth and brushed off some crumbs from Danny's spot. Maybe they should think about getting a smaller table. Maybe, then, it wouldn't seem like someone was always missing.

A single tear seeped from the corner of her eye and spilled down her cheek. She rubbed her face and took a deep breath. She had to stay strong for Sol, for Danny, but it was hard, so hard, to accept the will of God.

C.J. Fitzpatrick wiped down the dry erase board and scanned his classroom. "Looks like a wrap for the year, Tucker." His yellow Labrador retriever stared up at him with large dark eyes. C.J. stooped down and unhooked Tucker's service jacket. "You're off-duty, buddy. School's out." He patted Tucker's large head. He adored that dog. Tucker had been bred to be a guide dog for the blind, but was career changed because he was considered "too much dog"—a euphemism for a dog that was hard to handle. C.J. had been volunteering for Search and Rescue when the organization called him and said they thought they had a prospect for an SAR dog. They were right. Tucker was the best SAR dog C.J. had ever worked with—this dog was wired to work. He would go to any lengths for a Find.

C.J. and Tucker had rescued many lost people over the past two years. Most were Live Finds, but not all. He knew that would come with the territory of SAR, but it was still a terrible blow when he and Tucker found twin five-year-old boys last fall, too late, after a twenty-four hour search. The boys had wandered off while their parents were setting up camp. One boy was found first, early into the search. He had fallen down a steep ridge and hit his head. It took another nineteen hours to find the other boy. C.J. shuddered. The boy must have wandered in circles because his trail—his scent path—was scattered in all directions. C.J. finally found him quite a distance away, badly dehydrated and in severe shock. The boy was airlifted to a hospital, but pneumonia had set in and he died a day later. C.J. couldn't shake that experience off.

Tucker licked his hand, as if sharing the thought.

"Come on, Tuck, we need to get over that. We win some and we lose some. We *know* that." He walked over to the window to see if Jaime had arrived yet.

His thoughts drifted to the argument they'd had this morning. They'd started the day off on the wrong foot. But what had triggered it? He had just asked her if she was packed for the trip and she snapped at him. He had stepped in mud

26

and he hadn't even seen it. Where was safe ground anymore? All that he was wondering was if she needed him to take her suitcase out to the car, but she assumed he was nagging her to get ready. Jaime was so tense about this trip. He sighed. Lately, Jaime was tense about everything. The past few months, things seemed to be unraveling between them. He couldn't remember the last conversation they'd had that didn't end with Jaime upset with him, or worse still, silent. He could feel them drifting, drifting, and he didn't know what to do about it.

"C.J.? Yoohoo, are you there?"

C.J. spun around to find Eve, the principal's receptionist, standing by his desk with an envelope in her hand. He gave her a warm smile. "I'm sorry, Eve. I was just daydreaming."

"Here's your paycheck, darlin'. I already locked up the office and thought you might have forgotten about it." She put the envelope on his desk and turned to go, then came over to give him a hug. "Have a very merry Christmas, C.J. You deserve it. Especially after being nominated for the district's Teacher of the Year award. What a Christmas this is going to be!"

Sol told Zach to finish up in the barn while he and Danny went up the hill behind the farm to check the trap he had set yesterday for a pesky bobcat. He wanted to check on it before the storm hit. He told Mattie he thought there would be a good chance of outsmarting a hungry cat in a winter storm. Mattie watched her husband and son climb the hill until they were swallowed by the falling snow. The air was raw and piercing, and dozens of chores awaited her inside, yet she lingered still. She drew in a deep breath, smelling the cold that pinched her nose and the acrid smoke from the chimney that rose into the sky. She lifted her face to the snow, tasting it on her lips, letting its coldness sting her flushed face. Shivering, she gathered her shawl closer to her and went up the porch steps that led to the kitchen.

Mattie walked through the silent house. She always found it unsettling to rattle around in a house meant for ten. Five empty bedrooms. Too quiet. Too empty. Maybe, she thought, they should move. Far away from here. Into town.

Upstairs in her bedroom, a dimming afternoon light slanted through the window. She sat helplessly on the edge of the bed, a shirt of Sol's that she should iron for Sunday church hangiong limp in her hands. She had so much to do, she really shouldn't give in to taking a rest, but she felt a bone-deep weariness and didn't have the energy to fight it. What was more and more distressing, she didn't seem to care. She felt tears coming on. What was *wrong* with her? The doctor said she should be feeling better after a month or so, but she didn't. She felt just the same. Worse, maybe. What was happening to her sense of peace, her happiness? What was happening to her?

Her head itched as it often did after a day of wearing her starchy prayer cap. She pulled out the pins that held the cap in place and set them on the nightstand. The pins released her hair and she thrust her fingers through it, rubbing her scalp. She picked up her brush from the nightstand and took a moment to indulge herself, crossing the room to sit in the rocker by the window. She brushed her hair slowly, a hundred strokes, the way her mother taught her. How many times had she sat in this rocker? She had rocked Danny as a baby to sleep in this rocker. When she woke in the night, she often sat in it, listening to the evening songs of nature—the throaty song of bullfrogs, the violin scrape of crickets' wings, the clap of a thundercloud. Sol thought she was crazy to get up out of bed in the night—sleep was precious to him. But what she really loved was having time alone with the Lord—time that passed sweet and slow. It was her time for praying. And there were times when she felt God talking to her. Not like a person might talk, but a sense, a prodding. An idea would pop into her head—an insight or a solution to a problem. And then a sweet peace would flood her soul. She knew it was the presence of God.

But no longer. Since she had miscarried, God had gone silent, so silent. And in her soul, there had been only emptiness left behind, an emptiness that felt hard and cold as stone. She moved through the days as best as she could, but she could summon only a pale shadow of the faith that had always steadied and comforted her.

Her brush was full when she finished, a thick nest of pale silk, all the luxuriance of pregnancy slipping away as her hormone levels readjusted. Looking at all that hair in the brush made her want to weep. The world had become so very fragile. She slammed the brush on the arm of the rocker. *That's enough,* she said sternly to herself, blinking away the tears. She'd been paralyzed with grief, too full of sorrow even to weep. *That's enough, Mathilda Zook Riehl.*

She should go downstairs and iron Sol's shirt. Sol and Danny would be home soon, wondering where she was. She should go. In a moment. The breath eased out of her in a soft sigh. Her head fell back and she drifted off to sleep.

"A marriage unwraps slowly." Jaime said the words aloud as she left the pharmacy and drove toward C.J.'s school.

She had heard that phrase uttered on *Oprah* recently, and it seemed to be meant for her. That's just what had been happening with her and C.J.—their marriage was slowly unwrapping. "It's time for a radical change," she said to the rearview mirror. "It's as simple as that." She had practiced this speech dozens of times over the last week, after finally deciding she was going to accept her father's suggestion to move to New York City and sign with a photography agent friend of his. By the time she reached C.J.'s school, she was so tightly coiled, she ached.

She pulled into the parking lot of the junior high where her husband worked as a math teacher, and parked next to his yellow jeep. She glanced at her wristwatch: half past four. *Perfect.* For once she wasn't late! They were going to drive straight to her father's house in the city. The plan was to fly to Miami early Christmas morning to embark on a weeklong Caribbean cruise with her father. It was just what they needed.

A knock on her window made her jump. It was C.J. She quickly turned on the ignition to lower the window.

"I was starting to worry about you, driving in this snow," he said.

An expression of genuine concern filled his dark brown eyes. That way he had of looking at her, as if she was the most beautiful woman in the world when she knew she wasn't—it always made her knees go weak. Today, it made her feel like an emotional nutcase. How could he be thinking of having an affair with another woman and yet be so warm and loving to his wife? She couldn't process it. She turned back to face the steering wheel. "We'd better get going. If we hurry we can stay ahead of the storm."

"I thought we'd take the jeep."

She shook her head. "I want to have the GPS system so we don't get lost."

He hesitated. "Jaime, I have Tucker."

Jaime leaned over the open window to face the large coffee-colored eyes of the gigantic yellow lab. He was peering at her, standing by C.J.'s knees. "You said you were going to leave him with the principal."

"Al couldn't take him. They're going to his sister's house for the weekend and she's allergic to dogs. But he did say it was okay to leave your car here for the week. He said the lot would be locked up."

Jaime frowned. "There's got to be somebody else. What about that Eve woman?" *That she-wolf who is preying on another woman's husband?* She sneaked a sideways glance at C.J. to catch his reaction.

"She's got company staying with her for the holiday. I called and made a reservation at a kennel near your dad's house. It shouldn't be any problem. Your dad doesn't even have to know."

"My new car is the problem! Hair on the seat and drool on the windows and—"

"Then we'll take my jeep."

Jaime looked at the yellow jeep. She hated that jeep. She used to love it, used to imagine that this was what it felt like to be on an African safari. But now, it embarrassed her. The shocks were shot, you couldn't hear one another, the heater didn't always work, and Tucker would have to sit between them on the front seat. Plus, she would miss her beloved GPS system. "No. Just put a blanket down." She flipped up the trunk of her car so that C.J. could get a blanket. While C.J. settled Tucker into the backseat, Jaime set the GPS system for the street name the doctor had given her for the Amish family.

"Want me to drive?" C.J. asked.

"No thanks. I . . . I have a quick errand to make as we head out of town."

He climbed into the passenger seat beside her and touched her arm briefly. She tensed, lifting her chin to look straight ahead, and put the car in gear. C.J. withdrew his hand as if he had touched a hot stove. They fell silent as Jaime drove through Main Street, under white holiday banners that stretched from side to side of the street with cheerful greetings: "Seasons Greetings!" "Happy Hanukkah!" and "Happy Kwanzaa!"

As she turned onto a side street, C.J. said quietly, "When did wishing someone a Merry Christmas become politically incorrect?"

She shrugged, and turned her attention to the homes that lined the street. It wasn't quite dusk yet, but many houses had turned on their outdoor Christmas lights. The neighborhood looked like they must be having a contest to out-decorate each other: one had an enormous plastic Santa Claus in a plastic sleigh, pulled by eight plastic reindeer. Another was practically covered with blinking lights. She thought she might wind up with epilepsy if she lived across the street from that house.

C.J. shifted in his seat and turned to her. "A kid said the funniest thing to me a minute ago. I had an envelope sticking out of my shirt pocket and the kid asked what it was. I told him it was my paycheck and he said, 'Yeah? Where do you work?'" He chuckled to himself. "I love middle school humor."

"Did you deposit the check?"

C.J. rolled his eyes. "No, Jaime. I didn't have time."

Jaime groaned. "That means it won't get deposited until next week, and then the money won't be available for a few days past that. C.J., this time of year, we have so many bills to pay. We have Christmas gifts and—"

"Your credit card debt. Your cell phone payment." He reached over and picked up the edge of her scarf. "And let's not forget Burberry scarves."

"Don't. Start." She frowned. "I work just as hard as you do."

"At this rate, we're never going to be able to save enough for a house."

"You could have accepted my father's offer to provide the down payment."

"Let's not go there." He turned toward the window and was quiet for a while.

She glanced over at him and wondered what was running through his mind. He was usually pretty talkative. Had they already exhausted all neutral territory?

"I'm thinking I might start tutoring after school and weekends. Eve said some parents have been asking her about it."

Eve. *That* Eve. "You're trying to make me feel guilty." How incredibly trite that C.J. would be tempted to cheat on his wife with a woman named Eve. The original temptress! She glanced at him. She wondered if C.J. was in love with Eve. She wondered whether he would ask for a divorce soon. *That's what men do. They leave when they have someone new to go to.* She knew that from watching *Oprah*. From watching her dad.

"No, I'm not trying to make you feel guilty. But we need to face facts."

Which facts? Jaime wondered. *Yours or mine?* Should she confront him? No. Not now. Not today. Not on Christmas weekend. And maybe . . . if things worked out the way she hoped, if she could persuade him that they needed a radical change . . . maybe she wouldn't even have to.

C.J. was waiting for a response from her, but before she could get her words set into order, the GPS system told her to make a right.

"This doesn't seem like the way it was described to me," she said, under her breath.

"Did you set it correctly?"

"Of course I set it correctly," she snapped, turning right.

C.J. peered at the map on the GPS screen and looked skeptical. "If it doesn't feel right, why would you trust a piece of technical equipment over your gut instinct?" His placating tone was rimmed with an edge of exasperation.

She clenched her jaw. She knew that question wasn't just about directions. That question was a perfect metaphor for the differences between them—C.J. followed hunches, especially in his Search and Rescue volunteer work with Tucker. Jaime relied on reality. Equipment. State-of-the-art digital photography.

It was odd—they met three years ago. He was taking a class to become qualified as a volunteer in Search and Rescue and she was doing a freelance assignment to take pictures of the training sessions for the SAR website. They started in the same place. How had they drifted so far apart?

The persistent voice on the GPS system interrupted her thoughts to tell her to turn left, so she quickly veered left. They were heading away from town and into a much less populated area.

"Jaime, what kind of errand did you say you needed to make?"

Tucker popped his big head over the front seat and C.J. gently pushed it back.

"I just have to drop something off at a person's house."

"Whose house?"

"It's . . . a long story. Please be patient for a few minutes."

Then they were silent. Stilted. C.J., who usually never ran out of things to say, seemed reserved, distracted. Finally, he closed his eyes and yawned. As his breathing settled into a rhythm, Jaime felt relieved, knowing he had drifted off to sleep. She wished she hadn't promised that ancient Dr. Engel to deliver this silly whistle. He made it sound like it would be easy to find, but he didn't realize Jaime had no sense of direction. In spite of the urgency she felt, she slowed down—partly because the snow was falling even harder. Partly because, despite everything, she was enjoying the scenery. She lived so resolutely in town that she had forgotten all this was out here—all this *country*. She used to drive out this way with her mother on sunny weekend afternoons. She recognized this area, despite the whirling snow. Blue Lake Pond spread out silvery blue to her left, and just a mile down the road was the most beautiful Amish farm she had ever seen, Beacon Hollow. She and her mother had always wanted to turn up that driveway and meet the family who lived there.

Five minutes passed. Then ten. It was taking all of her concentration to focus on driving. Jaime thought she knew where they were, but felt a slight panic when the GPS system told her to turn off a main road onto a one-lane road.

C.J. jerked awake. He blinked and looked around. "Where the heck are we?"

"Almost there."

"What? Something just isn't making sense, Jaime. You're driving west, into the countryside."

"I have complete confidence in this car and its Global Positioning Satellite system." At least, she usually did. She felt a twinge of unease as she turned onto a one-lane road that had more than a few inches of fresh, untouched snow on the ground.

Jaime glanced at C.J.'s hands—the way he had them clenched in his lap was a dead giveaway that he was trying hard not to tell her "I told you so." She was just about ready to turn the car around when the GPS system told her to turn right to reach her destination. She turned her windshield wipers up as fast as they could go, knocking fat flakes off the windshield, and practically let out a whoop of joy when she saw the numbers on the black mailbox. Voilà!

She smiled victoriously. Her GPS had not failed her. "See? I told you we were nearly there."

He stared at her like she had spoken in Chinese. She ignored him.

Jaime drove up a long lane, using the fence rails to guide her along the snow-covered road. When she reached the top of the lane, the sight nearly took her breath away. Before her was a farmhouse glowing with buttery lights, smoke from the chimney rising to the sky. A cozy, welcoming beacon in the storm.

"Where *are* we?" C.J. asked.

She pointed to the whistle that was on the car seat between them. "I just need to drop this off at the house."

His eyebrows arched in surprise. "Are you kidding me? We've lost an hour of driving time because you needed to drop off a toy? What could be so important about this toy?"

"What's so important?" Jaime repeated, anger lifting through her like a wave. Those words incensed her.

How was it that anything Tucker-related never seemed to be unimportant to C.J.? Slobbering all over her car, taking extra time to find Tucker's kennel—those inconveniences were just fine for C.J. But stopping by a farmhouse to drop off a forgotten whistle to a little boy—that didn't rank as important? "What do you mean by that?"

"I didn't mean anything by that, other than wondering why this toy seemed so important," he said, exasperated. "Oh honestly, Jaime. What's wrong with you lately?" He was obviously at the end of his patience.

She wanted to shout, *You're what's wrong. I'm what's wrong. This whole thing is wrong!* But she didn't say a word.

The blue of early evening had settled over the room by the time Mattie awoke.

She regathered her bun so that it stuck off the back of her head like a knob and pinned her prayer cap in place. Downstairs, she glanced over her shoulder at the grandfather clock that stood beside Sol's desk—after five o'clock. Soon it would be dark. Sol and Danny were late coming home. She knew Sol was careful with their boy, but she never quite trusted him to watch Danny as closely as she did. So much danger lurked in the wilderness: rabid wolves and black bears and coyotes. And now the bobcat was prowling around, stealing her chickens! Danny could so easily become lost in the woods or fall into those streams with their steep, slippery banks that meandered through their property. Water was her greatest fear. The Schrocks' youngest child had died last spring in just that way. These dangers were a constant thing, yet he was her baby no longer, and as Sol was always telling her, she couldn't coddle him forever.

Just this very morning, they sat at the kitchen table, sipping coffee, and watched Danny run outside to meet up with Zach. Danny pointed toward the house and said something that made Zach's head fall back in laughter. Zach bent over and swung his cousin up in the air. The morning sun glinted off their two strawberry blond heads and something broke inside of Mattie in a terrible gush of pain.

"He's growing up so fast on us," Sol had said quietly.

His words, an echo of her own thoughts, pulled her gaze away from the window. She shared the sorrow in his voice.

Already she felt she was losing Danny. To the world outside of her safe home, to the land he was growing up to love as naturally as he breathed the air and ran through the wheat fields and laughed beneath the azure sky. And she was losing him to Sol and to Zach, into that male world where mothers felt unnecessary, a nuisance.

Mattie added a fresh stick of wood to the fire, punching the coals to stir them up. She dropped the lid back on the stove with a loud clatter, then went to the window to see if she could find some sign of Sol and Danny. She let her forehead fall to rest against the chilled pane. Where were they? The worry seeped into her like cold from the glass.

She heard the sound of a car through the wind. Probably someone lost, needing directions. For a moment longer, Mattie stayed where she was, feeling drained of energy, hoping Zach would see them first and send them on their way.

Jaime threw the car into park and grabbed the owl whistle. "This won't take long." The wind whipped into the car as she opened the door, ripping the car door from her hand.

Heavy snow bit at her as she hurried up the porch steps. She had just reached the porch when she thought she heard C.J. yelling. Before she could turn around, Tucker bounded past her and jumped up on the front door, barking. Jaime grabbed Tucker's collar to pull him back as the door opened. She was relieved to find the Amish mother from the doctor's office. She had the right house!

"Here," Jaime said, teeth chattering, as she thrust the whistle in the Amish mother's hands. "Your son left it at the doctor's office."

She spun around, hurried down the porch steps, and stopped in her tracks, stunned. Her car had disappeared.

As Zachary Zook hung a horse harness on a peg in the barn, he could have sworn he heard a car pull into the driveway. A gust of wind swirled past him as he slid open the barn door, knocking off his black felt hat. There *was* a car! A fancy-looking red sports car with a black convertible top. As he bent down to pick up his hat, a blur in a red coat emerged out of the driver's side and dashed up the stone path to the farmhouse. In the next instant, a big yellow dog bounded out of the car, chasing the red coat. And then a man jumped out of the passenger side of the car and ran behind the dog, hollering for it to come back.

Zach looked back at the car and saw it start to move—in reverse—and pick up speed until it crashed through the fence and rolled down the hill, finally coming to a stop as its back tires slid into the pond that Sol kept stocked with trout. It happened so fast that Zach didn't even have time to think— he felt as if he were dreaming. The woman in the red coat started to scream and ran toward the car. Zach ran after her, yelling as loud as he could, his words ringing through the bitter air, his mouth exhaling a frozen cloud, but she didn't stop. The snow, in parts, was at least four or five inches deep. He finally tackled her right before she reached the pond. The dog caught up to them and barked at Zach.

"Let me go!" the woman called out in a muffled voice, facedown in the snow. "My car! My beautiful car!"

She struggled to try to get up, but Zach wasn't letting her go. He was pretty sure she was crazy and would end up drowning if he let her get near that half-sunk car.

"At least let me get my camera!"

"Where is it?" he asked, keeping her pinned to the ground.

"Front seat. Black bag! I have to get it before it gets wet! I need it!" She stilled for a moment and Zach released his grasp, slightly. By now the man had caught up to them. He stood staring at the car in the pond, stunned.

"If you promise to stay put," Zach told the woman, "I'll try and get it. But you have to promise me you'll stay away from that pond. One step in and you'll sink like a stone and I have no intention of rescuing you." He relaxed his hold but waited to make sure she wasn't struggling before he finally released her.

She scrambled to her feet and glared at him. "I promise, I promise! I'll stay put! Now go, quick! Before it's too late!" She pointed to the car.

"Jaime! You can't expect this poor boy to risk his life in a freezing cold pond just to get your camera!" the man said in a firm voice.

She looked Zach up and down. "He's no boy! He's a grown man." She glanced at the man. "And I didn't ask him to. He offered."

Despite these bizarre circumstances, Zach felt a warm glow of pleasure at being called a grown man.

"Somebody needs to get my camera! Or I will go in there and get it!" She took a few steps closer to the pond.

The warm glow Zach felt instantly vanished. She shocked him, this English woman. The way she was pointing at the pond, she seemed like a queen directing her faithful manservant. Queen Bee, Zach named her. He rose to his feet, found his hat, and put it back on, all the while watching her suspiciously. "You stay there. Right there."

The man started coming toward Zach, but he waved him off. At least Zach had boots on. The man was wearing loafers. "Just keep her away from the pond's bank. It's steeper than it looks."

The woman frowned but didn't budge. Zach walked carefully to the edge of the pond, grateful that the car door was above the waterline. He turned to look back at her to object, but she only pointed again to the car.

"I have to have that bag!" She walked a few steps closer to the pond until the man grabbed her arm.

"You stay put!" Zach yelled.

The wind was howling around them, but she actually listened to him and took a step back.

"Please! I have to have my camera."

It figured, Zach thought. Something stupid like a camera. He waded into the icy water, stepping gingerly so he didn't slip in the muck, and tried to yank open the car door. It wouldn't budge, so he grabbed the handle with both hands and pulled with all of his might.

As it flew open, he slipped backward, seat first, into the murky water. The shock of the cold hit him and his chest felt pinched for air.

Can't breathe. Can't feel anything. I'm paralyzed. I'm dying.

But then—a gasp! His breath came out in short, frozen bursts, and his chest rose and fell heavily as relief flooded through him.

I'm alive!

He pushed himself up onto his elbows, then slipped again as he tried to regain his footing.

The big yellow dog jumped into the water like it was a hot summer day, swam over to him, and planted himself, giving Zach the boost he needed to pull himself to his feet.

Zach tried to act fast before he turned into a frozen ice block. He grabbed the black bag, turned off the ignition, and practically leaped onto the shore. He threw the bag at the English man's outstretched arms and made a dash to the farmhouse.

Sol and Danny had just emerged from the woods that ran along the top ridge of the farm and stopped for a moment to look over the valley as it filled with snow. It was Sol's favorite spot on earth. From that vista, he could see from one end of his farm to the other. It gave him a deep-down satisfaction, that one speck on the planet. Even today, with the wind biting and the snow falling hard.

Danny tugged at his pant leg. "Mom will be upset."

Sol nodded. "You're right. She's probably ready to send Zach out on a search party for us."

They had gotten distracted by a gory sight at the bobcat trap. It took awhile to find the trap in the new-fallen snow, but when they reached it, Sol found that the trap had been tripped. The animal had gotten away, leaving behind its bloody stump of a paw. The bobcat had chewed his paw off to save himself.

Sol had crouched down to examine the paw, to identify it as definitely belonging to a bobcat. This particular bobcat was the craftiest one he had ever tangled with. It found its way into Mattie's henhouse on a regular basis, helping itself to plump hens. With the kind of winter storms they were due to have, he knew this cat would be looking for a meal. He set that trap just yesterday, thinking it would tempt a hungry cat.

He let out a soft sough.

"Dad, that's not good, is it? An injured bobcat?"

Sol looked up at Danny. "Nope. Not good at all." He was sure the jaws of the trap must have cut the bobcat bone-deep. It would be crippled and bleeding, struggling hard to survive. And vicious.

"I feel a little sorry for it." Danny looked to Sol to see if that was all right.

Sol nodded that it certainly was. Anyone who grew up around farm animals couldn't side with a bobcat in the long clash of species. But it was another thing entirely to know a creature was suffering.

"Should we tell Mom?"

Sol sighed. "I sure don't want to but I probably should."

Danny tugged on Sol's pant leg again, snapping him back to the moment at hand. Sol straightened up and started down the hill, bracing himself against the wind with Danny following close behind him. They took a moment to stop at the next ridge to look over the valley. Then, as they started down the hill again, Sol saw the headlights of a car drive up the lane and come to a stop by the house. They picked up their pace after they saw some people get out of the car.

Then Danny suddenly let out a yelp. "Die Kaer!" *The car!* He pointed down the hill, a horrified look on his face. The car was heading backward, fast, right toward the pond.

By the time they reached the pond, Zach was bottom first in the water, somebody's big dog was swimming toward him, an English woman in a red coat stood at the pond's edge yelling directions, and an English man was beside her, looking mortified. Sol hunted for any kind of branch or stick that he could hold out to Zach. By the time he found something that could suffice, Zach was up and slogging through the snow and ice to reach the edge, then running up toward the farmhouse.

Sol's bewildered gaze shifted from the dog, shaking itself and getting everyone splattered with cold water, to the man, who had a very apologetic look on his face, to the back of the woman in the red coat. She remained facing her car in the pond, sadly shaking her head. Sol was flummoxed, unsure of what to say or do next.

It was Danny who knew what to do. Danny went up to the woman and patted her back, like a parent consoling a child. "Es ist nur eine Kaer. Es ist nur eine Kaer." *It's only a car. It's only a car.*

As Zach hurried to the farmhouse before he froze like a popsicle, he rushed past Mattie, who held the door open for him.

"Get by the stove!" she ordered. She shut the door behind him, and blocked the blast of frigid air. She guided him to a chair by the stove and pushed him into it, yanking off his shoes and socks. His teeth started chattering as he felt the heat from the stove; it seemed like pinpricks on his hands and feet.

Sol came through the kitchen door next.

Over her shoulder, Mattie said, "Sol! Go get some dry clothes. Quick!"

Sol bolted up the stairs, two at a time.

Mattie started to unbutton Zach's shirt, but he shook his

head and jutted his chin in the direction of the kitchen door. Danny had come into the kitchen with the English couple and their dog; they all stood staring at Zach. Even the dog.

Mattie turned to the Queen Bee. "Would you get that afghan from the couch in the other room?"

The Queen Bee disappeared for a moment and returned with the afghan.

Mattie took it from her, then asked, "Would you mind turning around so we can get my cousin's wet clothes off?"

The woman flushed a deep red and spun around to face the wall, still hanging on tightly to her black bag.

Zach's hands felt like they were burning hot, they were so cold. Strange, he thought, how hot and cold felt like such similar pain.

"Come on, lift up," Mattie said. He raised his arms and she tugged his shirt up over his head. "There," she said triumphantly, as she tossed the shirt on the floor. She wrapped an afghan around his bare chest and he leaned closer to the stove to try to capture its warmth. "You've got to get those wet pants off, Zach."

"You t-turn a-around t-too," he chattered.

Mattie rolled her eyes and turned around. With uncoordinated, shaking fingers, Zach unhooked his pants and tried to yank them off, but he couldn't bend very easily, he was still so stiff and cold. Sol came down, just in time, and helped by pulling. Zach stepped gingerly into the dry pants Sol held at his feet.

Mattie piled more blankets on top of Zach and told him to stay by the stove until his teeth stopped chattering. With the wet clothes off of him, he was getting feeling back into his hands and feet. Warmth had started to creep over his body.

"Seems like a funny time of year for a swim," Sol said,

toweling off Zach's hair. "Even for you." He left the towel hanging over Zach's head.

Zach snatched the towel off and managed a grin. A good sign! His face was thawing. "You'll think it's even funnier," he tried to say though his mouth felt stiff, "when you throw out a line next summer, hoping for trout, and you end up reeling in a car."

He stole a glance at the Queen Bee—this woman who nearly caused him to freeze to death tonight. He did a double take when he saw what she was doing. She was holding the baby barn owl, rocking it gently, as calm and soothing as a seasoned Amish mother. Mattie and Sol and Danny were watching the girl too, plus the man who was with her. All five of them seemed surprised to see the tender look on her face as she gazed at the owl.

Suddenly, she looked up, her large blue eyes round with wonder. "Isn't it beautiful?" Her eyes shifted from Zach to Sol to Danny to Mattie before resting on the English man's. "It's just the most beautiful thing in the world."

C.J. was, as usual, the one who thought to start proper introductions, taking a bit of the discomfort out of the air. For that, Jaime was thankful. C.J. made noises about trying to call for a cab and Mattie dismissed his words with a wave.

"No one is going anywhere in this storm," she told him, setting two more places at the table. "Dinner will be ready in a few minutes."

The storm had hit with a vengeance in the last half hour. Whiteout conditions. The snow was blowing sideways and drifts were already piling up on the driveway.

Jaime handed the baby owl back to Danny. She fought back a growing desire to pull out her camera and start snapping pictures, but she knew that the Amish eschewed being photographed. She had always been fascinated by these people—an interest she had shared with her mother. She looked around the house, trying to memorize every feature. It was low-ceilinged with small rooms. Everything had a secondhand look—the faded linoleum, the crooked blue cover on the couch. The only item of value in the room seemed to be a distinguished grandfather clock that chimed every fifteen minutes. The kitchen, like the rest of the house, was unremarkable. A harvest table with ten painted wooden chairs. Simple pine cupboards that lined the walls. Pale green formica countertops, outdated by decades. It was really old-fashioned, complete with stacked firewood on the porch. But the house was orderly and clean and comfortable and quite nice in every detail. It reminded Jaime of the summer cottage that her mother had rented for a week each summer for the two of them. Life pared down, scaled way back. There was no TV, no microwave, no computer. Were the Amish happier, living with so much less?

An awareness bounced into her mind. There were no Christmas decorations. None! No Christmas tree in the corner of the living room, no cheerful presents, no gaudy lights hanging outside, no stockings on the chimney. It was two days before Christmas and there was not a single sign of it anywhere. She knew the Amish celebrated Christmas. But how? These were Jaime's thoughts as she looked around the room.

Mattie finished setting the table and turned toward them, a satisfied look on her face. "It's nice for us to have company."

"But we're intruding," Jaime said. "If we could just get to a phone, we could call for a tow truck."

"The phone shanty lost power this afternoon when a tree branch went down on it," Mattie said.

"Phone shanty?" C.J. asked.

"The only phones we're allowed to have are kept outdoors, shared by neighbors, in a shanty," Mattie's husband said, pointing a thumb at the window. "About a half mile down the road."

Jaime banged her palm against her forehead. "My cell phone! If I could just get to it, I could call."

Zach gave her a suspicious look. "And where would *that* be?"

"In my purse," Jaime said. "In the car. Front seat!"

"No," Zach said, shaking his head firmly. "No way. Not happening. N.O." He spelled the letters in the air as if he were writing on a chalkboard.

C.J. ducked his head, trying unsuccessfully to hide a smile. It annoyed Jaime to see how amused C.J. was by Zach's boldness. That boy wasn't just bold, he was downright rude. So much for the stereotype of quiet Amish children! And he looked at her with undisguised interest, as though she were some kind of curious wildlife. How old was he? Sixteen? Seventeen? It was hard to tell with his Beatle hairdo, floppy bangs hanging down his forehead.

By the way that boy was glaring at her now, it was as if he was daring her to ask him to go back into that pond and fetch her purse for her. What was his problem, anyway? She was more than capable of retrieving it herself. She'd done crazier things than dipping in an icy pond while trying to snap photographs of wildlife. Besides, she *had* offered to go in to the pond herself! *He* was the one who insisted that she stay on the shore.

Sol snorted. "By now, it's either sunk or frozen until April."

Jaime regarded Sol, not appreciating that sentiment. Earlier this afternoon, at the doctor's office, she admired what a gentle and loving father he was, but now, in his home, with these unexpected visitors, she wasn't sure what she thought of him. She could tell he viewed them with minimal tolerance, or at the very best, as an inconvenience. He had hardly said more than a word to them, and she caught him frowning at Mattie as she set two extra place settings. She was starting to think he had the personality of a prison warden. Stiff, grim, unsmiling. But she had to admit he was exceptionally good looking.

"You remind me of someone I photographed once," she told Sol. "A calendar model. Mr. September."

As soon as she said the words, she wished them back. She was afraid Sol was going to choke. His lips crimped together while his Adam's apple bobbed. C.J. pinched his lips together in a line, as if trying not to laugh.

Then came a burst out of Zach, a guffaw that would have put Santa Claus to shame. "Mr. September!" he cackled out. Finally, his fit of laughter broke off into helpless snorts.

Jaime's face felt beet red. She should have kept her mouth shut. Saying "Mr. September" out loud did sound ridiculous. From now on, she was just going to answer questions.

But Sol did remind her of Mr. September! Her best-paying freelance job to date had been to photograph college fraternity boys for a calendar used to raise funds for a charity. Shave off Sol's silly horseshoe beard, give him a styled haircut, and he was a dead ringer for that photo of Mr. September—a handsome young man with a head of thick dark hair, in jeans, leaning against a split-rail fence.

Mattie, Sol's wife, was shockingly plain. She couldn't be more than five feet tall, with pale skin and large gray eyes that seemed too big for her small face. Jaime doubted she weighed one hundred pounds with a pocket full of change. She wore her wheat-colored hair in a bun so tight it made Jaime's head ache just to look at it. Mattie was unremarkable, easy to overlook, yet something about her was compelling, like the hub of a wheel. Yes, that was it. She was the center of this family wheel.

Jaime looked out the window. It was so dark it was impossible to even see the barn anymore.

"I might be able to help," Zach said, more kindly. "I might have—" he glanced down at the table—"a way to get to the main road."

Danny blinked at Zach through his round eyeglasses. A fleeting look of panic passed over him. "Ich hab dei Kaer gelast springa!"

"Was?" Zach roared, as though something hot had been spilled on him. "Ich hab dich gsagt fa weg bleiva!"

"Kaer?" Sol asked, in a tight, clipped voice. "Was fa Kaer?"

Everyone in the room was quiet—extra quiet?—and all that could be heard was the sound of the wind gusting outside.

Zach glared at Danny and pushed himself away from the table, grabbed his coat, hat, gloves, and a flashlight, and rushed outside.

Danny's face lit up. "Waarde, Zach! Woch will ich kumme!"

Before Danny could scramble off his chair to join Zach, Mattie and Sol shouted, in unison, "Nee!"

Crestfallen, Danny slipped back onto his chair.

Zach had left in such a hurry that the door didn't shut tight, and winter came into the kitchen on a blast of arctic air. Sol hurried to close it. As he sat down at the table, he said something else to Mattie in Pennsylvania Dutch. All that Jaime could pick out was something about a car. Zach's car.

Zach had a car someplace—and Jaime knew enough about the Amish to know that he wasn't supposed to have a car.

And Sol was *not* happy. Mattie looked extremely uncomfortable, caught between loyalty to her cousin and her husband.

Oh. My. Gosh. Mattie knew about the car! Jaime could see it in her eyes. *She knows!* Mattie suddenly became elevated to a person of intrigue to Jaime.

In a calming voice, Mattie said something to Sol in Dutch. Jaime guessed it was probably something close to, "Not now. We have company. We'll talk about this later." Then she turned to Jaime. "Is there someone who's expecting you tonight? Is someone worrying about you?"

Jaime exchanged a look with C.J.

"We were headed to Jaime's father's home," C.J. offered. "We're supposed to fly out on Sunday to go on a cruise over Christmas with her father." He put a reassuring hand on Jaime's forearm. "I think he'll be able to figure out that the storm is creating problems for us."

Jaime's stomach did a flip-flop. They *had* to get there in time to make the cruise. They just had to! This was the very first time her father had invited Jaime to spend a holiday with him. She had such hopes for this Christmas together, that it would be the first of many.

Danny cocked his head and whispered loudly to his mother, "Why would anyone not want to be home for Christmas?"

Mattie rested a hand on his head, trying to still him for a moment.

Jaime wasn't positive, but she thought she heard Sol say, under his breath, "Only the English."

Sol took his time at the kitchen sink, washing up before dinner. His mind was far away, mulling over what to do with Mattie's cousin Zach. Lately, he was starting to feel some empathy for Eli, Zach's father. Eli Zook was a stern man who saw everything in black and white. No gray. Zach always had a knack for aggravating his father with multiple shades of gray. And Zach's friends were part of a wild gang—wilder than any Sol had joined during his late teen years. True fence jumpers.

In her quiet, persistent way, Mattie talked Sol into offering a home to Zach. She believed that doing so could keep Zach close to the fold. "Remember a saying my grandfather Caleb used to tell us, Sol?" she would ask him with her big gray eyes. "'Better to stop one paddle short than one too far.' If we let him go now, if we're all against him, it's like going one paddle too far. It's too much. He might never find his way back."

In the end, Sol buckled. How could he refuse her? Mattie always saw the best in others. *She saw the best in me, when I was just like Zach*. A foolish young man. Mattie even talked Sol into meeting with the judge who oversaw Zach's court case. He was facing Minor In Possession charges for alcohol use. Since it was Zach's first offense, and Sol and Mattie were supporting him, the judge was willing to give Zach a steep fine coupled with a generous amount of community service hours to work off the misdemeanor charges.

Sol understood Zach's leaning toward the English world, no different than his own. And now, just like Sol had once done, Zach hid a car from his family. *How can I judge him when I did the same?* Besides, he had always been fond of Mattie's cousin. Zach's continual rebellious antics had been funny and irritating, but harmless, in a salt-in-the-sugar-bowl kind of way. If Sol would have ever had a brother, he imagined him to be like Zach. The feckless little brother, the talented one, the handsome one, the one no one could stay mad at.

Sol had plenty of conversations with Zach out in the barn about what it was really like out there, in that big world. He did his best to convince Zach that what he would gain wouldn't equal all that he would lose. Zach pretended to listen, but Sol could tell he didn't believe him.

Mattie scolded Sol once when he told her about their talks. She didn't feel he should be trying to influence Zach one way or the other. "It's his life to live, Sol," she said. "You just keep being an example of a fine man to him and leave the rest to God." That was his Mattie for you. She trusted God on everything, right down to the dollars in the bank.

The hot food had been served up on the table while Sol's mind was still out in the barn. He grabbed a dishcloth and dried his hands. As soon as everyone sat down at the table, Sol signaled for a prayer and bowed his head.

Lord God, he silently prayed, *I don't know why you would want us to have English houseguests on this weekend—Christmas weekend—but please give me the grace to tolerate them.* No, that wasn't quite right. The English fellow seemed to be a good sort. He really needed grace to tolerate her—the English woman. His thoughts wandered to other English girls he had met during his Rumspringa. They were all the same: shallow and worldly. She was a pretty one, this girl. It worried him to see the look Zach had on his face, about ten minutes ago, while he had watched the woman stare out the window at the storm.

Another dark cloud burst in on Sol's train of thoughts. He was starting to understand Eli's fear that Zach would turn his other children against the church. Sol had assumed Danny was too young to be noticing Zach's sloppy work habits—late weekend nights, falling asleep during church. Just a few days ago, he found Danny with a pack of cigarettes. Danny had unearthed Zach's stash, hidden in a barn rafter, and was fingering a cigarette, sniffing the tobacco. It made Sol furious to think Zach was smoking in the barn. The *barn*, of all places! And tonight, he discovered that Danny had known about the car and hadn't told him about it. That he had even turned it on and left it running! What else was Danny picking up from Zach? Six-year-old boys were naturally curious and Danny was particularly observant.

Mattie gently nudged him under the table and Sol, embarrassed, realized he had gone lost in his thoughts again. *Oh Lord*, he hastened to add, *thank you for the provision of this fine meal. Amen.*

He cleared his throat and tipped his head up, giving up a grin as he saw Danny try to slip that biscuit-colored dog a piece of pork. What he saw next gave him a start—the dog refused the pork. Its large brown eyes were fixed on the English fellow.

"Tucker knows not to eat unless I give him an OK," C.J. explained. "It's part of his training as a service dog."

"I didn't even think about what your dog might need for dinner," Mattie said. "I have dry dog food in the pantry. We keep some handy for strays."

"*We* don't," Sol said. "My wife does. She feeds the birds, stray cats and dogs—"

"Lost people too," Danny interrupted.

C.J. looked relieved. "That would be fine, if you don't mind. The bag of dog food I brought is in the trunk of Jaime's car." As Mattie got up, he added, "Not now. He can wait." He pointed to the floor and the dog collapsed onto the floor, burying his nose in his paws.

Sol had never seen such a well-behaved dog. He was worried the dog would go after Danny's barn owl, but other than an investigative sniff in its direction, he ignored it, as if he didn't expect to be here long so why bother making friends? "Is he always that good?"

C.J. looked down at Tucker and stroked his head. "He's a fine dog, but he's still a dog."

Sol picked up the mashed potatoes and passed the bowl to C.J. "What do you mean, a service dog?"

"Tucker and I volunteer for Search and Rescue," C.J. said, scooping some potatoes on his plate. "For the sheriff's department."

"That's your job?" Danny said. "I'd like that job."

C.J. laughed. "No. Just in my spare time. My full-time job is being a math teacher at the junior high."

"I'd rather be searching in the woods with a dog all day than stuck in a classroom," Danny said.

C.J. grinned. "I love Search and Rescue. SAR, they call it. In fact, that's how Jaime and I met. She was photographing the training exercises. Jaime works as a photographer. The best in the state of Pennsylvania."

Jaime blushed. "I'm not. Not by a long shot." She speared a piece of meat with her fork. "It's really quite interesting to see how the dogs are trained. You'd love watching it sometime, Danny." She took a spoonful of the chow-chow onto her plate. "What is this?" she asked, pushing it around on her fork.

"Chow-chow," Mattie said. "It's an Amish dish. A staple, really. I think I could count on one hand the times I've sat at supper without chow-chow."

"But what's in it?" Jaime asked.

"Pickled vegetables," Mattie said, looking up at the ceiling as if she was reading a recipe card. "Cucumbers, cauliflower, carrots, green peppers, lots and lots of vinegar. And sugar."

"How did it get a name like chow-chow?" Jaime asked.

Mattie shrugged. "Nobody knows."

"How'd you get a name like C.J. and Jaime?" Danny asked.

"Danny!" Sol warned. He gave his son the look, but Danny's attention was riveted to the English guests. Danny couldn't help asking questions. It was just the way his mind worked. He had such a curiosity about most everything, much more than Sol did at that young age. And he was so unusually bright! Sol often worried what choices Danny would make as an adult. Would he remain in the church? Would a farmer's life be enough for him? But that was a worry that could wait for another day.

"C.J. are my initials," C.J. said. "Stands for Charles Joseph. Kind of a mouthful for my mother to holler out when I got into trouble so it was shortened to C.J."

Danny snorted. "My dad was named Solomon because his father wanted him to be as wise as King Solomon."

Sol tousled his hair. "And that's why I prefer being called Sol. Lowers expectations." He exchanged a fond smile with Mattie. She often told him that Solomon suited him and he knew it didn't.

Danny's eyes were turned to Jaime, waiting for an answer to his question. He didn't give up, that boy of his.

"I was named Jaime after my father, James, because I was a girl. My father told my mother that one child was his limit . . . and he wanted a boy." Jaime spread butter delicately on the roll before taking a bite.

An awkward silence covered the kitchen. Only the English, Sol thought, would put a limit on a family. They didn't understand what he knew to be true—that every child was a blessing from the Lord. Why would anyone want to limit blessings?

When they were nearly done eating, Zach blew into the house and took his seat at the table, sullen and mad. He scowled at Danny and didn't offer to drive the English folks anywhere. No matter where he had hidden that car, it would be tire-deep in snow by now. Sol had to stifle a smile at the thought of the car left running by Danny. It was wrong of his boy to mess with the car, but Sol couldn't help but find pleasure at the thought of the car's engine freezing up in this storm. *Too bad! Ha!*

After watching Zach wolf down his meal, Sol offered a silent prayer to give thanks back to God for daily bread. He stood and plucked his coat from the wall peg. "Danny and Zach and I will go check on the stock."

"Sol, let me help you." C.J. grabbed his coat and hat from the wall peg. "Let the boys stay in the warm kitchen. Heaven knows Zach earned a reprieve."

Zach frowned and Sol knew why. It bothered him to be referred to as a boy. He was itching to be considered a man.

Zach pushed back his chair and stood. "I'm fine." He rubbed the top of Danny's head. "Let him stay."

"But I need mice!" Danny looked at his father with panic. "To feed the owl!"

Sol nodded. "I'll bring your mice. When I get back, we'll finish up that puzzle."

"Stay out of the pond," Mattie told Zach, lifting her eyebrows with an innocent look. "That's your only dry coat."

"I'll do my best," Zach said. He cast a glance in Sol's direction with just a wisp of mischief coming through. "If I forget, I'm sure Mr. September will remind me."

Sol tried to doff Zach's hat, but Zach expected it and

stepped closer to the door. He braced himself before heading out the door, pausing for a moment with his hand on the door handle. He took a deep breath and rushed outside. Sol and C.J. followed behind and Tucker dashed through the door before it closed.

As Mattie collected the plates, she basked in a feeling of sweet relief. How kind of that English fellow to offer help so that Danny could stay inside! It was much too cold outside for a little boy. But her relief went deeper than that. She could hardly bear having Danny away from her. She knew it wasn't right to feel so anxious about a child. She couldn't seem to help it and the thought troubled her. So many things troubled her. Things she couldn't tell anyone about. Not her mother or her sisters-in-law or her best friend, Carrie. Not Sol, either. Everyone expected Mattie Riehl to be the strong one and she wouldn't disappoint them. But oh, she longed to spill all the troubling thoughts that had plagued her lately.

Who could possibly comprehend, though? Who could understand that she was turning into someone she hardly recognized? Going to baby showers for her friends and sisters-in-law and feeling so terribly envious that they were popping babies out right and left, while her arms remained empty. Everyone was kind, but she knew they pitied her. She knew that she was now defined by her faulty womb. *Mattie's the one having difficulty. Something's wrong, poor thing.*

This time, conceiving after so many years, she was sure she would finally have another baby. When the bleeding came, it nearly undid her. She couldn't get out of bed for days. The doctor told Sol it was to be expected with so much blood loss, but she knew it was more than that.

She gathered every dirty dish and utensil from the table, as well as the English woman's plate that still held leftover chow-chow. She must not have liked it; she left it untouched on her plate. The English man ate everything.

Mattie had shooed away an offer of dishwashing help from the English woman. She could tell the woman didn't have much experience in a kitchen, and she could clean the dishes in half the time without someone asking her what to do or where a bowl went.

When Mattie finished with the dishes, she glanced over at Danny, sitting cross-legged on the floor with the barn owl in his lap. That was when she noticed that Jaime was crouched on the floor, just a few feet away from Danny and the owl, snapping pictures of them with that fancy camera.

Mattie reached out and pulled the camera out of Jaime's hands. "While you're in our home, I expect you to respect our ways," Mattie said in a sharp tone. As soon as the words left her mouth, she wished them back. The shocked look on her son's face shamed her. What was the matter with her? What made her snap at a stranger like that?

Jaime rose to her feet. "I'm sorry. I thought . . . they made such a sweet sight."

Mattie took a deep breath. She laid the camera on the table and sat down. "We Amish, we don't want our pictures taken."

"I thought it was different with children," Jaime said. "Before they were baptized. I thought it was just adults who were off-limits."

"Ask, first," Mattie said, more gently.

Jaime tucked a stray curl behind her ear. "Of course, you're right. I'm sorry. I'm a photographer. That's what I do. It's who I am. I just . . . I looked over at them and in my mind, I saw the picture. I just . . . I did what I do."

Mattie softened. "So this piece of metal is why you sent my poor cousin into that frigid pond?"

Jaime's eyes went wide, then she burst into a laugh when she saw that Mattie was teasing. She reached over and picked up the camera. "I would've dived in after it myself, if he'd only let me. I've only had this camera for a few months. It takes amazing pictures." She let out a sigh. "C.J. thinks I take better pictures with my old camera. He thinks I rely too much on the bells and whistles of this digital camera and not enough on my instincts."

Mattie leaned forward in her chair and clasped her hands together. "That's the first time tonight you've stopped looking so worried!" She pulled a chair out for Jaime. She found herself fascinated by her, this English woman. She wasn't like the Amish women Mattie knew, who were so careful about what they said and how they said it. This woman just blurted out whatever was on her mind. She had a way of looking right at you as if she was searching for something, hoping you had the answer for her. Jaime had held the camera carefully, as gently as if it were a robin's blue egg. It was precious to her, Mattie could see that. "Your husband must have a lot of confidence in you, thinking your way of seeing is better than a camera's."

An odd, uncomfortable look came over Jaime's face. What was it? Guilt? No. No . . . it was misery. Whatever did this English woman have to feel miserable about? Mattie thought the woman was going to share what troubled her, but then Danny coughed and the woman looked startled, as if she had forgotten he was there. And the moment passed.

Mattie went over to Danny and put a hand on his forehead. "Maybe you should put on a sweater."

"Mom, I'm fine."

"A sweater is something a boy wears when his mother is chilly," Jaime said.

Mattie looked at Jaime strangely.

"It's a saying. Something my mother used to say."

Mattie turned back to Danny and pointed to the sweater lying on the bench by the door.

Danny sighed, deeply aggrieved, but got up and put it on. "Can't I go out and help Dad?"

"No," Mattie said. "Not in this storm. I'll whip up hot chocolate and popcorn."

Satisfied, Danny went into the other room to start working on the puzzle.

Mattie watched him for a moment, then asked Jaime, "You said you were going on a trip with your father for Christmas. Where's your mother?"

Jaime winced, as if that was the last question she had anticipated. "She passed away."

Mattie reached out and covered Jaime's hand. "You must miss her very much."

Jaime closed her eyes for a split second. "Oh, I do. I would give anything to have another day with her. Just one day."

The strange note of weariness in her voice touched Mattie's heart with pity. She gave Jaime's hand a slight squeeze. Then she turned her attention to filling a pot with milk from the refrigerator before setting it on the burner. She poured vegetable oil in the bottom of a large kettle, added popcorn kernels, and swished them all around so they would be covered in oil before covering the kettle with a heavy lid. She stayed by the stove to shake the kettle as the kernels popped. She could feel Jaime's eyes on her, watching, taking it all in. Was her kitchen so very different from an English person's kitchen?

"So, Jaime, tell me about taking pictures." She glanced back at her.

Jaime looked at Mattie curiously. "What do you want to know?"

"I want to know why you like to take pictures." She heard the oil start to sizzle and gave the kettle a shake. She glanced over her shoulder at Jaime. "What was the first picture you ever took?"

A sweet look came over Jaime's face. "My mother gave me an inexpensive throw-away camera when I was seven. I snapped shots of everything a seven-year-old thinks is fascinating: spiderwebs, a cat's nose, a flower." She smiled. "My mom had the pictures developed at one of those one-hour places. I wouldn't leave the store so we waited by the counter until the pictures were done." She shook her head. "Those pictures were terrible, just terrible, but I was hooked from that moment on."

"Why?" Mattie asked. "Why were you hooked?" It was plain to see how much this meant to Jaime. Her entire face lit up as she talked about taking pictures.

"There is nothing more satisfying than capturing that one, perfect image," Jaime said. "I enjoy the trial and error of it all, tinkering with various positions and lighting and composition until I get it right. I love the variety of the work. And I guess the photographs make me feel like I matter. As if I had something to say, and I can use photographs to say it." She shook her head. "Probably sounds silly to an Amish farmwife."

Mattie was quiet for a long moment. A few kernels of popcorn started to pop so she held on to the kettle's edges with two potholders and gave it a hard shake. "What kinds of pictures do you most like to take?"

"Outdoor photographs—of nature, of wildlife. I enjoy the unpredictability of photographing the outdoors. So many things are out of your control—lighting or posing—but there are times when I capture something that just takes my breath away."

"Sounds challenging."

Jaime sighed. "It can be. Even indoors, in Sears Portrait Studio." She clicked something on her camera and the lens folded up. "Photography is a very competitive field. It's hard to stand out. I don't want to be just another two-bit photographer. I don't want to be ordinary, you know?"

Mattie pinched her lips together in a line, trying not to laugh.

"What?" Jaime asked, confused. "What did I say that was so funny?"

"Now *that* . . . that does sound silly to an Amish farmwife. Wanting to not be ordinary. We do everything we can to avoid standing out. You English . . . you do everything you can to draw attention to yourself."

"But . . . that's not what I mean. That's not what I'm like."

"No?" Mattie asked. She looked over at the wall pegs, filled with black coats and black hats and her own black bonnet. Jaime's red coat hung on the end peg. "You wear a bright red coat, for one. If that's not someone who wants to stand out in a crowd, I don't know what you'd call it."

Jaime frowned. "I guess what I meant is that I want to do something with my photography that makes a difference. I want to feel like this is what I was meant for, the reason I'm on this earth." She looked up at Mattie. "Haven't you ever felt that way about anything?"

Mattie was quiet as she took the kettle of popcorn off the burner and dumped the steaming popcorn into a large bowl.

She drizzled melted butter on top and shook salt over it before setting it on the table. Danny came into the kitchen and sat on a chair to stir the popcorn with a large wooden spoon. Mattie stroked his hair. Motherhood was firmly ensconced in Mattie, anchored deeply in her body. "Yes," she told Jaime. "Oh, yes. I have felt that way."

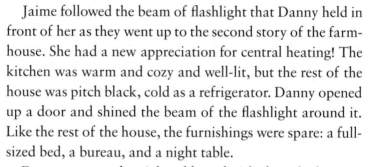

Jaime followed the beam of flashlight that Danny held in front of her as they went up to the second story of the farmhouse. She had a new appreciation for central heating! The kitchen was warm and cozy and well-lit, but the rest of the house was pitch black, cold as a refrigerator. Danny opened up a door and shined the beam of the flashlight around it. Like the rest of the house, the furnishings were spare: a full-sized bed, a bureau, and a night table.

Danny went to the night table and picked up the lantern. "Mom won't let me use matches, but you can light this yourself."

Jaime went over to him. "Show me what to do."

He pulled off the glass hurricane and turned the wick up on the base of the kerosene lantern. "Here's where you light it."

Jaime tried to light a match, but her fingers were clumsy with cold. After watching her try three tries, Danny took the matchbox from her and lit a match, held it to the wick, then put the hurricane back on the lantern base.

"Mom said to show you where the bathroom was." He picked up the flashlight and went back out to the hall.

She followed behind him. "Do you use a lantern in your room?"

"No. Just a flashlight. She worries I'll read too late and a lantern would catch fire."

"Most moms tend to worry a lot."

Danny nodded solemnly before opening another door. He beamed the light around a small bathroom with a big porcelain tub, a sink, and a toilet.

Indoor plumbing! Jaime didn't really know what to expect inside an Amish farmhouse, but she wasn't sure she should expect indoor plumbing. Hallelujah!

"There are towels on the hooks. Mom said she put a nightgown for you on your bed and a new toothbrush in the bathroom." He turned and walked down the hallway back to her bedroom. At the door, he scrunched up his small face, peering at her intently through his glasses. "Maybe my mom doesn't need to know that I lit the match."

"We'll keep that our secret. After all, you were just helping me, Danny. Thank you."

He gave her a shy smile. "Thanks for bringing my whistle back. My dad made it for me after we found a snowy owl's nest. They migrate here for the winter. They can find their prey by listening for it, even under the snow."

"No kidding? I would love to photograph a snowy owl."

"Sometime, I'll take you to see a bald eagles' nest. It's made of sticks, with clumps of grass inside to line it like velvet. It's as big as—" He looked toward the door to see if anyone was coming. "It's as big as a 1983 Toyota Corolla. The eagles moved in and built the nest last spring and no one knows they're here. I'm not telling anyone."

"Why not?"

An uncomfortable look passed over Danny's face. "If the game warden knows, he'll post no trespassing signs up on our property but those are like an advertisement for folks. They'll come with their binoculars and telescopes and cameras and set up camp." He pushed his glasses up on his nose.

"Eagles are the most amazing birds you ever could believe. They have a wingspan," he stretched his arms as wide as he could, "as big as this. Eight or nine feet." He sat on the bed. "But if you come with me you'll have to wear glasses. Did you know that predators go after the eyes of their prey? Even spitting cobras. They have perfect shots that spit poison right at an animal's eyes—"

"Danny!" Mattie's voice floated up the stairs.

He jumped off the bed at the sound of his mother's voice and gave Jaime a wave as he slipped out the door. Mattie did keep a close watch on her son, Jaime noticed. Almost as if she didn't want him out of her sight for more than a moment or two. Jaime closed the door as Danny's light footsteps jumped down the stairs. That boy was intriguing. He was small for his age but talked like a docent at a natural history museum. She found herself unexpectedly drawn to him. He reminded her of . . . a little of herself as a child. Serious, studious, more comfortable with adults than with other children. But unlike Danny, she was always trying, trying, trying to fit in, like a square peg in a round hole. She always felt she was missing something essential, something everyone else in the world seemed to have.

A father.

She thought of all of the lies she had told when she was Danny's age to excuse the inexcusable absence of her father: He's a spy for the CIA. He's a scientist who studies melting glaciers. He works six months at Antarctica, six months at the Arctic Pole. And her favorite: he's in the Federal Witness Protection Program. Her ruses worked for a few years, but soon, the kids grew wise to her. And far less tolerant of someone who didn't fit their mold. Her mother dragged her to a counselor once, concerned that Jaime had no friends. The counselor asked Jaime why she didn't just tell kids the truth.

The truth was simpler, but far less intriguing—and it was too painful. Her father didn't want to be a father. Or maybe he just didn't want to be *her* father.

She wondered if other children picked on Danny the way she had been picked on. She was always happier out in nature, among wildlife, where no one made fun of her, especially about her hair: Woody Woodpecker. Medusa. Cardinal head. Her mother told her to pay no mind to others, that one day she would love her hair. Well, she was now at the advanced age of twenty-five and she still hated it.

C.J. loved her hair. He said it was the first thing he noticed about her—that day when she was assigned to photograph the Search and Rescue training. He had made her feel beautiful for the first time ever in her life. He would tangle his hands in her wild mop of hair and implore her to promise that she would never cut it. She would laugh and tell him he was crazy, but she would never promise that she wouldn't cut it. Someday, she knew she would find the right haircut for her mess of hair.

And that's just what happened. Her father appeared one day, not long after her mother had died, treated her to a haircut at a very expensive salon, and voilà! Her hair looked the way she had always wanted it to. Short, straight, asymmetrical. It looked amazing! At least, for the rest of that day. She had never been able to style it the way the hair salon had. And the new short style made it surprisingly high maintenance, requiring frequent haircuts. Trying to make curly hair straight required expensive bottles of mysterious potions and sprays. Plus a vicious-looking hair iron.

The look on C.J.'s face when she came home from the hair salon that first time still irked her. He looked betrayed. As hurt as if she had brought home a lover. But she had never promised not to cut it. After all, it was her hair!

And it wasn't long after that she noticed how often he brought up the name of Eve. *That* Eve. That home-wrecker.

A month or so later, he started staying late to work on a project with her. A project. What kind of project would a junior high math teacher and a school receptionist have in common? The thought would not recede: C.J. was having an affair.

Once, she almost asked him how he felt about Eve, but the words clogged in her throat like a dammed-up river. It was just as well. What if C.J. said he cared for Eve, what would happen then? It was better not knowing, she decided. It was better to hope somehow she was wrong than to know she was right.

It's sad, Jaime pondered, how the feeling of falling in love doesn't last forever. She thought back to how wonderful things had been with C.J. when they were first dating, over three years ago now. He had courted her with a slow, persistent patience, showing up at Sears Portrait Studio, solid and steady, week after week, offering a fistful of flowers or some other corny gift, the pleasure on his face so real that she could not bear to turn him away.

She'd never met anyone like C.J. He was funny, charming, self-deprecating. As they zipped around streets in Stoney Ridge—a town she had grown up in and he was new to— he pointed out things she never would have noticed on her own. Well, that wasn't entirely true—she did notice things. But they were *things*. The unusual architecture of an old, neglected house. C.J. would look at the same house and ask her what she thought the couple was like who first built the house. Were they young or old? Did they build it large to accommodate a growing family? "Can't you just hear the quiet echoes of their voices, Jaime? Children, now grown, playing in the backyard? A mother and father on the front porch, sipping lemonade on a hot summer night?" And the funny thing was—she started to see what he saw. How an object related to a person. C.J. was all about relationships. At that point, Jaime's photography jumped a level in subtlety and sophistication; even she could see the difference.

She was driving to a freelance assignment on a winter morning, just after a snowfall, and came across three Amish quilts hanging on a clothesline. Nothing else was around, just those vibrant, brilliantly colored quilts against a white back-drop. She pulled over, put a roll of fresh film into her camera, and used up the entire roll. She took them back to develop in the makeshift darkroom in her apartment—a seldom-used bathroom. She adjusted the lighting so the vibrant patterns of quilts would pop against the crystalline detail of the snow.

Later, C.J. studied the picture. That was when he said to her, "The composition of this photograph is pure genius, Jaime. You should send this in."

"To what?"

He handed her an entry form for a national photography contest sponsored by *National Geographic*. "To this."

"That's crazy!" It was something she had never considered, although she wasn't sure why not. Failure, she supposed. She couldn't bear the thought of failing at something she cared so much about. But he convinced her to send it in.

She wondered if C.J. ever regretted it, knowing that con-test would become the point in their relationship when the ground shifted. As real as if they had been tectonic plates that lined up against each other until an earthquake split them into a yawning crevasse. That's what winning the contest felt like—an earthquake.

Because that was the moment her father first began to notice her. That was the point when he started to call her, to invite her to New York, to provide guidance to help build her career, to surprise her with thoughtful gifts. To act like a father.

Jaime picked up Mattie's nightgown but decided she was so cold she didn't want to get out of her clothes. She piled quilts on top of the bed and shivered as she climbed between the chilly sheets. The sheets were white and crisp, the pillows so soft it was like sinking her head into whipped cream. Even still, she lay in bed, stiff and cold. How did the Amish live like this year-round? Didn't they know what they were missing? Electric blankets. Central heating. She would never get to sleep. It would be another night where she tossed and turned, waking exhausted and cranky.

She heard C.J. and Sol and Zach come inside, stomp the snow off their feet, and laugh over something. They seemed to hit it off. Not that it surprised her—everyone liked C.J.

As her eyes adjusted to the dark, she noticed the pattern of the quilt on the bed. It was an enormous white star with rays spread out across a field of midnight blue. In the murky light, the star looked jagged and broken as if it had fallen from the sky and shattered. She turned over on her side and punched up the pillow under her head. The wind whistled like a pipe, blowing shrill. The walls moaned in deep bass, resonating in her bones.

Sol's voice, laughing as he and Danny worked on a puzzle together, floated up the stairs. Mr. September. As she listened to him laugh and tease his son, she adjusted her assessment of him once again. There was more to him than she had thought there was at dinner, when she assumed he was a fellow all tied up in his own righteousness. There was more to all of them than she had first thought. These Amish weren't at all what she expected. A little odd, but oddly appealing.

Take Mattie. She seemed to genuinely want to know why Jaime was so interested in photography. Of all things for an Amish woman to ask about! She never would have thought she and Mattie would have such an instant rapport as they did tonight, after the men left to go to the barn. As they talked in that little kitchen—a homey, comforting place, accompanied with the soft gurgling of the oil in the lamp as background music—Jaime felt the freedom to open up about her life in a way she didn't with anyone else. It wasn't long before the two women were talking to each other about all kinds of things. It felt good to talk to another woman. Mattie listened, really listened to her, and didn't try to fix everything. She just empathized. At one point, Jaime couldn't believe she was here, talking so intimately with a stranger. It was odd but thrilling too, like confiding in a person you met on a train or a bus.

Jaime even told Mattie about her father's offer to set her up with an agent in New York City. "It's amazing, really, to think my father would help me at all," she confided in Mattie. "He used to say that photography is a hobby, not a career. And that a woman needs to be able to support herself."

The puzzled look on Mattie's face surprised Jaime. For a moment, Jaime had forgotten how different their worlds were.

When Mattie asked how C.J. felt about giving up his teaching job and his Search and Rescue work to move to New York City, Jaime said they hadn't worked everything out yet. That wasn't technically true. They hadn't worked anything out yet, because C.J. didn't know about it.

"You see, I didn't really think I wanted to move until this week. Then, suddenly I did. I really want to live in New York. I want to sign with this agent and do some big-time photography." She knew she couldn't stand another year being stuck in Sears Portrait Studio, photographing unhappy babies. Or crying toddlers in ballerina tutus. Or little girls dressed up in so many ruffles they looked like Victorian valentines. Or cats. So many people wanted their cat in their annual Christmas picture! This morning's cat with Mrs. Peterson did her in. Jaime had scratches all over her hands from that hostile cat. After the shoot, she went straight to the manager's office and told her she wouldn't be coming back after Christmas. She quit!

Jaime expected to see judgment in Mattie's eyes. Instead, she saw understanding. Mattie covered Jaime's scratched-up hand with her own and said, "It can be hard to say important things to the person in our life who matters the most."

Jaime flipped onto her back and looked up at the ceiling. It was so dark outside that no moonlight shone through the clouds, but she could see the ceiling was painted the same glossy color as the walls. Pale blue.

Mattie had made an odd, poignant remark that struck at Jaime's heart—it penetrated so deeply that she excused herself and went to bed.

"Poor communication doesn't disconnect souls," Mattie said. "It's the disconnected souls who poorly communicate." Then she added, "But love is so much more than words."

What did *that* mean? *Does she think I'm disconnected with my soul?* Suddenly, Mattie's words became clear to Jaime. *She thinks I'm disconnected from C.J.*

Me? It's C.J. who is disconnected from me. He's the one who's cheating! If it hadn't happened yet, it wouldn't be long before it was an actual affair. Twice during dinner tonight, C.J. mentioned that Eve woman. Twice! Once when they were talking about Tucker, and he said how Eve loved Tucker so much that she took him out for walks at lunch. And then, later, he thought Eve might enjoy Mattie's recipe for chow-chow. When Mattie asked him who Eve was, he said she was just a co-worker. *Just a co-worker.*

Mattie might be insightful—surprisingly astute—but she obviously wasn't clairvoyant. *You missed that one, Mattie. It sailed right past you.*

Just a few hours ago, Jaime had thought of Mattie as a plain woman. The plainest of Plain women. Yet tonight, in the soft lantern light in the kitchen, Jaime reframed that opinion. Mattie was intriguing. She was not a beautiful woman, but yet she *was*, because she was completely herself. She was slender; she carried herself with a dancer's grace and reserve. But there was something else she carried, as obvious as her plum-colored dress and white prayer cap: a mark of strength and wisdom, of motherhood.

Jaime knew she ought to feel sorry for Mattie; her father certainly would. Mattie lived in a drafty old farmhouse and had a husband who worked as a farmer. They would never make much money. She had never been on an airplane in her life. Or a cruise! But the three of them—Mattie, Sol, Danny—they were a happy family. Unlike Jaime's father, Sol was home. And when he wasn't, they always knew where to find him. Mattie's home was filled with peace, comfort, and constant, safe companionship. Jaime felt a growing tickle of admiration for these Plain people.

Whenever Jaime had thought of her father—there had been no one to picture. It had always been just Jaime and her mother, Connie, and random checks from her father that would arrive without any note included. There was never anyone to help them out, no man in Jaime's childhood. She grew up with an empty spot inside, a part of her missing. A hole. A *black* hole.

C.J. had come from a completely different kind of home.

Simple but loving. Like the Riehls'. C.J.'s solidness was one of the qualities that drew Jaime to him. He was a rock. He had a genuine interest in the lives of people. He remembered their names, their children's names, their situations—if they were thinking of buying a new car, or if they were caring for an elderly parent, or if their dog had just died. This was stuff he cataloged in his brain. It was unusual how much he remembered, how much he truly cared. People lapped it up. Everyone adored C.J.

She was the opposite—happier to be out in the woods, behind the lens of a camera, observing, alone with her interior life. When people asked her too many questions, she felt like she was being pecked at by chickens.

Downstairs, a peal of laughter burst out of Danny. Jaime wondered what had made him laugh. There was something about that little boy that touched her. The way he looked, so small and thin and solemn. The way he talked and asked big questions and the brightness of his laughter that was like a glow on his face. She felt as if . . . well, if she ever had a child, she would want him to be like Danny.

What was she thinking?! She didn't even *like* children! And worse—they didn't like her! Babies and children always cried when they were in the studio, no matter what tricks she used to get them to smile in their picture.

She had come to bed early to try to get much-needed rest. She wished she had thought to put those stupid sleeping pills in her coat pocket instead of her purse—which was in the car. She was sure it was going to be one of *those* nights, when her mind spun and her brain pleaded for the relief of sleep but her body would not oblige.

Jaime punched the pillow again and rolled over, watching the snow whirl through the undraped window. She felt an aching sadness that she couldn't understand. A hollow emptiness. What would fill it?

She didn't know.

The house was quiet. That was perhaps the most noticeable difference, C.J. thought, between living in town and living in the country. The absence of noise. He slipped into the full-size bed next to Jaime, careful not to waken her. Tucker jumped up on the bed right behind him and C.J. pushed him down toward the footboard before the dog bounced on Jaime. He rubbed Tucker's head and whispered to him to lie down. Tucker peered at him solemnly before curling into a ball and releasing a big sigh. Then C.J. stretched out. He never would have believed he would end this day—the day before Christmas Eve—needing refuge at an Amish farmhouse. In the dark, he smiled. He had a new appreciation for Mary and Joseph, seeking shelter and finding it in an unlikely place, before the very first Christmas.

When Jaime's car went into the pond, he felt horrified—both at her carelessness but also at what it meant. It wasn't that he minded missing a day with Jaime's father—just the opposite. The thought relieved him. And it wasn't his fault! Surely, James MacComber couldn't blame a storm on C.J. that was walloping the entire Eastern seaboard.

James was convinced Jaime had married beneath her, which was ironic because he had just become interested in getting to know his daughter. James made no secret of how he felt about C.J. A junior high teacher barely scratching out a living in a small town in southeastern Pennsylvania—who had turned down a promotion to become an assistant principal. He'd never forget the afternoon when James called and

Jaime told him C.J. had turned down the opportunity. There was dead silence. C.J. counted down in his mind: *5, 4, 3, 2, 1.* And then the grenade blew up! "He did *WHAT?*" C.J. heard James's voice echo across the room. He knew James could never understand that C.J. loved being a teacher and had no desire to get into administration. No indeed, it didn't bother C.J. to have a bona fide reason to spend one day less this Christmas with his father-in-law.

But how could they impose on this Amish family? Mattie, in particular, couldn't have been kinder about the intrusion. She could sense C.J.'s discomfort. As she handed him a pair of her husband's pajamas to wear, she told him, "God doesn't make mistakes. He has a reason for bringing you here."

He thought it must be wonderful to have that kind of solid faith. This year, he had started attending church and tried talking Jaime into going with him. So far, no luck.

"Are you asleep?" Jaime whispered.

He turned onto his back. "I thought you were. I was trying to be quiet."

"How could anyone possibly sleep with a dog the size of a humpback whale taking over the bed?"

C.J. grinned and lifted his head. "Did you hear that, Tuck? She called you a whale." Tucker let out a soft snore at the foot of the bed. "He forgives you. He's not easily offended."

"Hmmph," Jaime murmured.

C.J. folded his hands behind his head. He stretched out in the bed, careful not to disturb Tucker, and wriggled closer to her. "Maybe this is how the Amish have so many children. Small beds and cold winters."

"Not this family."

"No. When we were in the barn, Sol told me that Mattie had just miscarried."

Jaime stilled.

C.J. looked over at her. "He said that was why they were at the doctor's today. That they had met you there."

"Danny left the whistle at the doctor's office."

"Mind telling me why you were at the doctor's?"

She blew out a deep breath. "Just a prescription I needed."

"For . . ."

Jaime turned to face the window. "For some sleeping pills. In case I needed them for the trip."

C.J. sat up and leaned on his hands, peering over her at the window. "Looks like Mother Nature might have a say in that. I'm not sure we'll be able to get a tow truck out here tomorrow."

"What? It can't take long to get those roads plowed."

"Sol says another storm is right behind this one. A storm from the north is blowing through. It's supposed to bring twice as much snow." He stretched back on the bed. "Funny thing is, I don't really mind. I kind of like this. It feels like a chance to slow down and think about things. Important things." He leaned up on one elbow to face her. "We've needed time like this. We've needed it for a long while. There's a lot we need to talk over."

They lay in silence for a time, listening to the wind, to the crack of a frozen tree branch that snapped off in a gust.

It was easier in the dark like this, to talk. "It seems as if we're growing apart, Jaime, and it worries me. I know the last year has been difficult, with your mother passing. And suddenly your father is in your life. I still feel badly about that weekend when your father was visiting and I had my first . . . unsuccessful search." He couldn't say it aloud. Deceased Finds. "The timing was just bad." It had taken him a long time to get over that event. He had felt like such a failure. He couldn't even talk about it with Jaime. He raised his hand to stroke her cheek, but then thought better of it. He let it fall without touching her.

"It's not your fault. It's not anybody's fault."

Were they talking about the same thing? These days they were like two planets, orbiting without colliding, but not drawing any closer either. "What isn't?"

"Drifting apart. Sometimes, it just happens."

Why did her voice sound so settled, so defeated? "Jaime, this is no way to have a marriage."

She was quiet. "No. It isn't."

"We can do better."

"I suppose you're right." Her voice was flat and the answer was quick, like she didn't even have to think about it. What was the undercurrent he heard in those words? Disappointment? Resignation?

The comfort of the darkness gave way to a deeper unease and a chill went through C.J. He didn't want to hear any more. "We'd better get some sleep." He rolled onto his side, away from Jaime. "I love you, Jaime."

"Me too, you, but sometimes love is just not enough."

C.J. lay awake, unable to sleep, running over their conversation in his mind. He'd wanted to connect with Jaime, to have a moment when they understood each other, but his good intentions had spiraled into distance.

The wind smacked against the house, startling Mattie awake. She was disoriented for a moment, aware only of the cold that lay thick and deep around her. Then a fresh gust slammed against the wall, making it moan. Or was that Danny?

She slipped out of bed to go check on him in his room. She touched a hand to his forehead; his skin was warm and damp. He had Sol's thick eyelashes, which curled against his cheek when he slept. There was no more beautiful sight than her child asleep. She loved Danny so profoundly, his perfect little body and all the complexity it contained. *My child*, she thought. *My son.*

He stirred and mumbled a few words that she couldn't make out before he settled back into his dreams. What did a six-year-old boy dream about? A scooter? A pony? A cart to go with it? Those were the things he wanted most, and he made Mattie set timelines. Can I have a scooter when I'm seven? Can I have a pony when I'm eight? Danny was charging through his childhood, eager to be as old as Zach.

"Slow down, sweet boy," Mattie whispered, and covered him.

He was so capable, so independent, so smart. He had taught himself to read when he was three, he knew his addition and subtraction tables up to ten by age four, he kept a list of rare animals that he and Sol spotted—bog turtle, piping plover, Indiana bat.

Slow down, sweet boy.

As soon as he learned to talk, a day with Danny was one long conversation, filled with unanswerable questions. Why is the sky blue? How far away is the moon? Did you know a blue whale's heart is as big as a small car?

Slow down, sweet boy.

She stood for a minute in the wind-echoing room with her hand on the doorknob, moved by Danny's smallness, by all the ways she would not be able to protect her son in the world. She closed the door softly and stopped by Zach's room when she noticed the light under the door.

She knocked gently and poked her head in the door. "Can't sleep?"

Zach lifted his book. "In the middle of a good chapter." He yawned.

She took a few steps inside and leaned against the wall, crossing her arms against the cold. She and Zach were more than ten years apart in age, but they'd always had a special closeness. He was right on the precipice of leaving the church. She sensed the restlessness within him. The knowledge didn't trouble her, not like it did her uncle Eli. The way it bothered Sol. She felt about Zach the way she used to feel about Sol—she saw the man he could be. She knew Zach would make the right decision . . . in the end, if he could have a little room right now to think it all through for himself. But instead of giving him some margin, Zach's parents had cut him off. In their minds, he had two choices. Settle down and become baptized, or leave now. All that his parents had succeeded in doing was to drive Zach further away.

"How bad off is your car?"

He closed the book. "Bad. Couldn't even start it. The ignition was frozen. The key broke off."

"I'm sorry," she said, meaning it. Danny should not have been fooling around in that car. When did he get into it, anyway? She watched him like a hawk. "I can't remember a storm like this one." Every hour, the temperature dropped a few more degrees and the windchill stirred the air to make it even colder.

"Bet those English folks are feeling the cold," Zach said with a devilish grin. He didn't look at all sorry for them.

"They seem very grateful to be here."

Zach shrugged.

"I had a good talk with the English woman while you were all out in the barn. She's not what she seems."

Zach put his book down. "What's that supposed to mean?"

"I suppose that she might have seemed a little selfish, at first, letting you go into that cold pond. But there's turmoil in her life. She reminds me of a lost little lamb. I think she's trying to decide something important."

"And what would that be? Which new shoes to buy?"

Mattie smiled. "I'm just saying . . . that maybe God brought them here for a reason. Maybe we can help them."

"Mattie, she's not one of those stray puppies that follow you home. You can't fix everybody."

"Just . . . give her a chance. We should be pitying her for her lostness. Maybe . . . you could be a little . . . nicer."

He rolled his eyes at her and she smiled, then she left. As she walked down the hallway to her bedroom, she caught a reflection of herself in the night-blackened glass window, illuminated by the glow from her flashlight. The woman who stared back at her was not herself at all, but a stranger who looked so thin and so sad. She put her hands up to her face and squeezed. *Stop! Stop feeling so sad!*

Behind her, Sol slipped his arms around her waist. She felt the tickle of his beard as his lips grazed her neck. "Were you watching our son sleep again?"

She leaned her back against him and covered his hands with hers. "I thought I heard him call out."

Sol's hands were warm, large, and comforting. He had been so patient all these years, so reassuring. Always optimistic that they would have more children. She raised his hand and kissed his palm, strong, rough with calluses, marked with lines. She placed his hand on her heart, held it there.

"You worry too much about the wrong things, Mattie." He kissed the top of her head. "He's nearly seven years old. You hardly let him out of your sight. He needs to be doing much more around the farm with me. Like other boys his age. Most eight-year-olds can do the work of a man."

She stiffened. "Danny's *not* like other children his age."

"That's why we need to give him more practical experiences. More chances for him to learn skills."

"That's not what I meant. He's small for his age. He can't do the kind of work you and Zach do. It isn't fair to expect so much."

"That's not what I'm saying. It's time that we give him more responsibility. More independence."

This wasn't a new conversation between them. It went round and round, like a loop. It was the same discussion that they'd been having for two years now. Sol said their boy was trying hard to grow up and she shamed him with her fussing. She felt he didn't understand the way Danny was. The way she felt.

Sol turned her around to face him and pulled her close. She felt the press of his beard against her neck.

"I know you're hurting, Mattie. I know how much you want to fill this house with children. But we still need to raise the boy we have into a man."

Mattie was still for a long time, listening to the wind, her head resting on Sol's chest. She knew, deep down, that he was right. He was a good husband to her, a good father to Danny. But her desire to be a mother was a physical, painful hunger. She could think of nothing else. Tears pricked her eyes, and her throat ached. A deep sense of loss rose up in her, so forceful, woven from month after month of spoiled dreams for a baby. Tears were slipping down her cheeks. "It's not fair," she whispered.

"It's not fair," Sol agreed.

He kissed her then, full on the lips, and pulled her close. She pressed her cheek against his, taking in his scent and warmth.

"Come to bed," he invited.

She nodded and put her hand in his.

Christmas Eve

Zach woke with a start and jumped out of bed. He had promised Sol he would check on that laboring ewe before dawn. He threw on his clothes, shivering as the cold fabric touched his body. He tried to creep quietly down the stairs so he wouldn't wake Sol. Mattie's husband liked to think that they were cut from the same cloth, but Zach knew better. Sol acted more like a father to him than a cousin. He didn't want to risk a disapproving look from Sol if he forgot that ewe. He got plenty of those dark looks from his own dad.

When he reached the bottom step, he was surprised to find Queen Bee sitting at the kitchen table, fully dressed, with the yellow dog sitting beside her. The lantern on the table created a glowing circle around her. Queen Bee's hair, which had been loose yesterday, was now held in a stubby ponytail, and little ringlets fell around her neck. Wide blue eyes the color of a summer sky. He had definitely admired her looks—as soon as he recovered from the dip in the pond—but this morning, she looked different. Cheerful and sweet and pretty. And pretty old, he guessed. Maybe twenty-five or thirty.

"Uh, we won't be having breakfast for a while," he told her.

She shrugged. "I couldn't sleep. Thought I'd just come downstairs and read for a while. It's warmer down here."

Zach glanced at the grandfather clock. "I need to go out to the barn and check on the animals." He headed to the door, then turned back. "There's a ewe that might be lambing soon." He noticed Jaime's camera, left on the table. "If you want to take a picture of something special, a lamb born on Christmas Eve . . . I wouldn't object." He reached for her red coat, plucked it off the wall peg, and held it out for her. He wasn't really sure why he thought she might like to see the newborn lamb. He supposed it was Mattie's comment that Queen Bee seemed like a lost little sheep herself.

The delighted look on Jaime's face warmed him. Ah—he was a sucker for attractive women. It was one of the complaints he had about being Amish—the women were just so bland looking. His thoughts drifted to Susie Blank, his particular friend, and he felt a twinge of guilt. Susie wasn't bland. She was pretty, with thick chestnut hair and emerald green eyes. And she had an effect on him that could make his thoughts travel down dangerous and wicked paths. He stole a glance in Jaime's direction as she put on her coat and hat and gloves, then tucked her camera inside her jacket.

She looked up at him and gave him a dazzling smile. "Ready?"

Nope. Cute as she was, even Susie Blank did *not* hold a candle to this English woman.

A blast of cold air shocked Jaime when Zach opened the door. The cold stung like needles on her face. She debated if she really wanted to bother venturing out in that bitter, black cold only to end up in a bitter, black, and cold barn.

When she started to complain, Zach turned to her and said, "Are you always this whiny?"

Pretty much, she thought. At least this past year. But that was going to change, starting now.

Tucker didn't seem to mind the cold at all. He bolted out of the door and disappeared into the dark to find a private place to relieve himself. Zach paid no mind to either of them. Suddenly remembering Jaime, he pointed out the holes he made with his boots so she could follow in his tracks. The flashlight he held in front of him cast a bright circle onto the snow.

Just trying to walk across the yard to the barn felt like climbing a mountain, the wind was pushing that hard against them. Finally, Zach pulled open the barn door, yanked Jaime in, and shut it tightly just as Tucker slipped around his feet and into the barn.

At the sound of someone coming, the animals stirred in their stalls, murmuring and huffing. It was pitch black inside, as dark as if they were in a box. Zach pulled off a glove and lit a match against the wall. He shielded the flame with his other hand and took a few steps to where a lantern hung on the wall. The match blew out before he had time to light the wick, so he set the lantern down, crouched next to it, and lit another match. The wick sputtered, then caught, splaying light into the shadows.

Jaime's eyes watered at the sour stink of sheep and cows and horses and pigs and hay and manure. She nearly gagged but fought it back; she was eager to photograph the birth of a lamb. Zach laughed when he saw her pinch her nostrils together. His smile, she thought, was like the sun coming from behind clouds. It was a dazzling smile. She watched Tucker, delighted by rich layers of earthy smells, make his way around the barn by sniffing the perimeters. A dog's paradise!

Zach walked over to the ewe's pen and motioned to Jaime to follow him. The two of them stood side by side, watching the ewe. Their breath came out in puffs of cloud, though Jaime felt better without the wind slicing through her coat.

"There," Zach said, pointing his chin toward the ewe. "See the shudder that runs through her belly? That's a labor pain."

The ewe's water had broken some time ago; the straw was littered with blood and birth mucus. The ewe dropped down on her front knees and lifted her bottom in the air. Her lips slipped back over her teeth, grimacing in pain.

"Can't you help her?" Jaime asked.

Zach picked up a piece of timothy hay. He dangled it from his lower lip and leaned against the rough boards of the lambing shed, crossing one foot over the other. "Nope. She's no amateur. She knows what she's doing."

The ewe raised her head to look at them with such a serene, gentle look despite her suffering that the sight took Jaime's breath away. She snapped a few shots of the ewe, hoping to capture the deep look in her eyes. It was haunting! She felt tears sting her eyes but fought them back. Lately her moods teetered precariously. They felt like a basket of fruit balancing on her head.

Zach plucked the hay out of his mouth and pushed himself off the shed wall. He took another flashlight and headed down the aisle of the barn, checking on each animal. Jaime remained transfixed by the ewe's stall, watching her body still as she prepared for each contraction that rippled through her body.

The ewe let out a deep moan and Jaime said, "Can't you do *something* to ease her pain?"

Zach emerged out of the shadows and looked at the ewe. "Pain isn't always a bad thing."

Oh, you're so wrong about that. Pain is a terrible thing. It chews up your insides and tears you apart.

He glanced at Jaime. "This kind of pain—this birthing pain—this is right and natural. It may hurt for a while, but soon, you'll see—she won't even remember it." His attention riveted back to the ewe. "Better get your camera."

Almost as if on cue, the ewe knelt down again and started to push. Jaime took picture after picture as the birthing sac pushed through the opening. Each time the ewe labored, a little black nose appeared—only an inch or two—and then disappeared. Finally, she gave a mighty heave and the lamb slid, bloody and sticky, into the straw. Zach jumped over the small railing and was right there to cradle the lamb. His fingers tore away the membrane from the tiny black nose. Jaime snapped frame after frame.

He picked up some hay to tickle the lamb's nose. The lamb sneezed, then gasped, then let out a loud, indignant *baa*! The ewe came around to sniff it, to make sure it was hers, Zach explained. Laughing, he collapsed into the straw, cuddling the bawling lamb in his lap. His mouth broke into a smile that blazed across his face like the explosion of light from a photographer's flash. He motioned to Jaime to come inside the stall, so she did as she continued to take pictures. She only stopped for a second when he asked if she was going to run out of film.

"It's digital," she said. "I have a huge card."

She was just about to show him how to view the pictures when the ewe decided the lamb must be hers and she let out some pleased-sounding bleats, nuzzling with her baby, nose to nose.

Lost in the moment, Jaime took more pictures. Finally,

as the lamb settled in to nurse, she put her camera away. "Amazing, how white the lamb is and how dark the ewe is."

"That's dirt on the old ewe. Sheep don't clean themselves off like other animals do. A cat can clean itself. So can a dog. A bird gets into a birdbath. But sheep? They get dirty and stay that way. They don't mind being filthy. They're not the brightest creatures." He gave a short laugh. "Probably why the Bible often refers to us feeble-minded humans as sheep." He leaned his back against the stall. "The Lord is my shepherd, I shall not want. He leadeth me beside still waters, he maketh me lie down in green pastures, he restoreth my soul." He gave her a shy grin. "Do more beloved words exist?"

Jaime didn't know how to respond. She was startled—floored—to hear words of Scripture spill from this teenager's mouth as easily and naturally as if he was talking about the weather. She had heard those words all of her life, yet they seemed so alive, so real, here in an Amish barn.

Zach didn't seem to be expecting a response, which was good because she didn't have one. She wasn't on speaking terms with God at the moment. For over six months now. She hadn't been, ever since her mother's random, senseless death.

Sol woke at dawn when he heard someone thundering down the stairs. He recognized Zach's loud footsteps—the boy would have insisted he was being quiet. Sol thought about getting up to go into the barn with him, but then thought better of it. Zach was up and would check on the ewe and the other stock, his own bed was warm, his wife was sleeping next to him. Why get up? He had woken often during the night, restless, hearing the wind that battered the house and shook the windows. He couldn't remember a blizzard like this one. Every hour, the temperature dropped a few more degrees and the windchill stirred the air to make it even colder.

But then he heard a loud bang. It would be just like Zach to leave a barn door unlatched. Just last week, he left the sliding door to the barn wide open and two horses wandered out and down the driveway. Mattie stirred as he swung his feet out of bed onto the cold wooden floor.

"Go back to sleep. I just want to check that a barn door didn't fly open." He leaned back to bundle her up in the covers and kissed her on the forehead. He grabbed his shirt and pants, threw them over his shoulder, and quietly left the room. He looked through the hallway window at the barn and saw light from a lantern shining through a small window. No door seemed to be open. Still, he was wide awake now, and it was chore time.

He went into Danny's room and shook him gently on the shoulder to wake up. "We've got choring to do, son." Danny groaned and Sol smiled. That boy of his could sleep through a tornado. "Up. I mean it." He waited until he saw Danny's feet slip out of bed and onto the floor.

Danny followed Sol into the bathroom and sat on the edge of the tub, rubbing his eyes and yawning, while Sol shaved. It was their morning routine. Then, like always, one question spilled out of Danny: "What makes soap start to bubble?" It was followed by another unanswerable question, then another and another. Sol craned his head around to look at him. Danny and his questions! Soon, Danny was talking in that excited way of his and kicking his heels against the tub. Sol lathered his cheeks with soap from the soft brush, taking pleasure in listening to his son. The razor blade slid in smooth, clean strokes against his cheeks.

For a moment the whole world seemed to be held, suspended: the start of a new day, the sharp scent of laurel soap, and the animated voice of his son.

Zach and Jaime stood there for a while, gazing at the ewe and the lamb. Tucker trotted up to investigate, sniff, and get a pat on the head from Jaime. Satisfied all was well, he disappeared into the recesses of the barn for more sniffing.

It was Zach who broke the silence. "What do you want to name the lamb?"

"Can I?" Jaime said. "Hmmm . . . let's name her Noel. It's French for Christmas."

"Noel it is." He pronounced it as a man's name. "She's a he." Grinning, he rose to his feet.

She flipped the switch on her camera. "Here, look at these." She showed him the pictures through the screen. He was fascinated by it and stood right behind her shoulder. There was one picture where he was holding the lamb and laughing. She looked up at him, wondering if he would object. "I can delete it if you'd prefer."

Zach only grinned. "What a good looker that fellow is." He wiggled his eyebrows. "Just don't go showing that one around at church on Sunday."

"Oh, we won't be here on Sunday," she said. "Later this morning, we'll be on our way."

"Think so?" Zach asked, in a tone that implied she was kidding herself.

She spun to face him. "Absolutely. This storm can't last forever."

"Maybe not, but the *Almanac* says another one is right

on its heels." He puffed out a big white cloud of breath to illustrate his point.

"What's the *Almanac*?"

Zach cocked his head. "*The Farmer's Almanac*. A book. Comes out every year. Something we rely on to tell us the weather."

"You're kidding, right?" She started to laugh, but then her face grew serious. "There are satellites out there, taking pictures of moving jet streams."

Zach shrugged. "I know about satellites. Amish aren't stupid, you know."

Jaime looked embarrassed. "I didn't mean—I just . . . I just can't believe that a book printed long ago could be more accurate than a satellite."

"Do they always get it right? Your weathermen."

A smile spread over Jaime's face. "No. They're right about half the time."

"Well, then, I guess the *Farmer's Almanac* isn't such a bad risk."

"So you really think another storm is on its way?" Her eyebrows knit together. "My father is expecting us. He planned this trip to the Caribbean for Christmas to help me through that first holiday without my mother."

"Where's your mother?"

"She died in a car accident about six months ago." She frowned. "My folks divorced when I was a baby. My father has been married and divorced . . . uh, let's see," she looked to the rafters, "four times now."

Zach's eyebrows arched, his mouth formed a silent O. She had shocked him and he didn't shock easily. It's not that all Plain marriages were perfect. Most were pretty happy, but he knew of a few couples who had troubles. Money troubles, usually. But they didn't just give up. Every couple knew what kind of commitment they faced when they wanted to marry. They married for life.

The ewe lay down on her side and the lamb cuddled in close beside her, practically disappearing under her woolly fleece.

"I don't know why I'm telling you all this."

Zach filled with warmth. He liked that she was confiding in him. "Maybe my cousin was right. Mattie usually is."

"Right about what?"

"Maybe the Lord brought you here this weekend for a reason."

"You make me smile—the way you talk."

"Good. You need to smile more."

She laughed and linked her arm through his. This, Zach decided, would forever be the moment in his life when he first felt like a man. Standing with a beautiful girl, with her arm entwined through his. Zach felt a sort of thrill when she touched him, and on the heels of that thrill was a worry. What was he thinking? She was married!

This was also when Jaime asked, "Zach, why aren't you living at home?" in a grave way, as though she knew there was more to the story than met the eye. And instead of giving his usual brush-off: "Just working for Sol," Zach expelled what felt like all the air from his lungs. "It's a long, boring story about a father and son."

She smiled gently. "I've got just enough time for a long and boring story."

It was the sincere and interested look in Jaime's face that opened the floodgates for him. He told Jaime things about the last year that he would never think of sharing with anyone else. About feeling so invisible to his father, so insignificant.

She seemed fascinated by what he was telling her. He had grown up as the middle boy in a family of eight children; no one had paid close attention to him, ever. He told her thoughts he had never shared with another, not even with his friends. They had all been raised to not stand out—how could anyone understand his need to be noticed?

Zach explained how he and his friends had been caught by the police with alcohol, and his father blew up. "He didn't even ask me if I had been drinking. He just told me to get out. Told me I would sour my younger siblings like a bad apple. Soft and rotted."

"Had you? Been drinking?"

Zach scowled. "Well, yeah, but that's not the point. One little mistake! And he tosses me out like I'm a piece of junk." He kicked at the ground with his boot.

Jaime's eyes went wide. "Really? One little mistake?"

Zach gave her a sneaky sideways glance. "Maybe two or three." Or a dozen. Getting into trouble with the law was the last straw for his father. After he had been charged with an M.I.P., his father had told him that he washed his hands of him and that the Lord God would see fit to deal with him now. It was well known that Eli Zook and the Lord God held similar convictions on nearly every subject.

"Your father sounds like an intimidating man."

Zach kept his eyes on the ewe. "He gives me the same sort of feeling I get in church, and not a little fear in it." He smiled ruefully. "I'm my father's middle son. Most of my life, I spent working beside him. I was born to work. That's all I'm good for, in his eyes. And now, no matter where I go, I'm surrounded by my father's family. It's been a burden."

Jaime shrugged. "Or a treasure."

Maybe both, Zach thought. A burden and a treasure. When

he had exhausted himself of all the frustration and anger and discouragement of the last year, she didn't say a word. "Now it's my turn to say that I don't know why I'm telling you this," he said.

"Maybe because I like to hear."

Jaime was a good listener. She did not automatically take his father's side, as Zach had expected. She was understanding his side; she was—still!—holding on to his arm. They just stood there in the peace of the morning, watching the ewe and her baby.

Finally, Jaime broke the silence. "Have you thought about leaving?"

"I've thought of nothing *but* leaving. The thing is . . . I love cars. Everything about them."

"Oh, me too! The smell of a new car is heaven."

He cocked his head at her. "I guess . . . I meant what's under the hood. The mechanics. The horsepower. The sound of a purring engine." They looked at each other. Her blue eyes matched his shirt. She was ridiculously, absurdly beautiful, and Zach looked into her blue eyes until he knew looking one more second wouldn't be good for him. It would be like eating too much chocolate.

He shifted his gaze and noticed her hand, resting on his arm. She had taken off her glove when she took pictures of the ewe. Her hand was so small! And so white. Impossibly soft and white. Her fingernails were painted dark pink; they looked like raspberries. *Enough!* he thought, and he may have actually spoken the word because when he glanced up at Jaime, she tilted her head and looked at him strangely, as if to say, *Enough what?*

He cleared his throat and looked away.

"Then, maybe a better question is, why do you stay?"

"Why?" Zach shrugged and kicked at a dirt clod on the ground. "It's hard to explain."

Despite the uncomfortable circumstances that brought him to Mattie and Sol's home, Zach felt himself growing attached to Danny. Danny followed him around the farm whenever he could slip away from his mother, wore his black felt hat tipped back on his forehead the way Zach did, saved cookies for Zach, he even started walking the way Zach walked— hands jammed deep in his pockets with a long gait. Last week, Danny told him, "I wish you were my brother." And Zach felt his heart grow three sizes.

To be adored? He loved it. A little kid affecting him this way? No one would have believed it.

<hr />

In the kitchen, Sol fed the fire in the woodstove. He shook down the ashes and threw in some kindling before tossing in a log. The new wood settled into the fire with a pop and a hiss. It pleased him that Mattie was still sleeping. She needed her rest.

Danny came down the stairs and went straight to sit on the backdoor bench. He pulled on his boots and coat, waiting for Sol. Together, they made their way through the snow to the barn. When they got inside, the big yellow dog greeted them as if he was the welcoming committee to a barn frolic. Danny ran to the lambing pen where Zach and the English girl were standing together.

"You've got yourself a Christmas lamb!" Zach said when he saw them, grinning from ear to ear. "Mom and baby, happy and healthy."

Danny climbed through the slats to reach the lamb. First, though, he patted the ewe and congratulated her.

Sol watched the lamb nuzzle against Danny. "I'm sorry I missed it." He was too. There was nothing so wonderful as the birth of an animal. Something he never tired of.

"Would you like to see pictures of the lamb being born?" Jaime asked.

Sol surprised even himself with a quick nod. Jaime unzipped her camera bag and flicked on a switch, then brought the camera over to Sol to look through the viewing screen. Mesmerized, Sol looked at the pictures, frame after frame.

"It's as if you're just inches away," he said.

Jaime continued scrolling through images. When Sol saw the pictures of Danny, sitting in the kitchen, holding the barn owl, he inhaled sharply.

"I'm sorry!" Jaime said. "I didn't know it was wrong, not until Mattie told me. I'll delete them."

"No," Sol said firmly. The answer came up deep inside of him. "No. Leave them." He looked up at the ceiling rafters. "Maybe . . . you could send those pictures to us sometime."

Jaime clicked off the camera and tucked it back in the padded bag. An awkward silence was finally broken by Danny.

"The owl! I need to see if there's a mouse in the trap." He leaped over the lambing pen, grabbed a flashlight, and ran toward the feed room. The sound of his footsteps echoed through the barn.

Jaime watched him disappear into the feed room. "I'll go help him." She hurried down the center of the barn. Tucker trotted behind her, tail up.

Sol's gaze was fixed on Zach. He saw Zach's eyes follow Jaime as she walked into the darkness. "Zachary," he said firmly. "No."

Zach shrugged and lifted his palms in the air, his eyes round with innocence. "What?"

"No." Sol shook his head. "For so many reasons, no."

Mattie rubbed a circle of frost on the kitchen window to peer outside toward the barn. She could see the lantern light streaming through cracks in the siding. She turned toward C.J., sitting at the table with a cup of coffee in his hand.

"Looks like they're still out there. Probably the ewe had her lamb." She wondered if Danny had dressed warmly enough. She thought she had heard him coughing, earlier this morning when Sol was shaving. But then, she hadn't slept well, and with the racket the wind was making, who knew if what she heard was a cough? Still, a sound woke her and then began the circle of endless worries. She blew air out of her mouth. *Stop. Stop, Mattie!*

C.J. stood. "I'll go out and help. I used to milk cows. I could squirt a stream of milk straight into the cat's mouth."

Mattie glanced at C.J., surprised by that comment. He wasn't nearly as tall as Sol, but he didn't look short either. A square-faced man with a cap of close-clipped blond hair and dark brown eyes and smooth-shaven cheeks. He wore jeans, a T-shirt, with a thick gray sweatshirt that said "Slippery Rock State University." He had a clean, friendly look about him. Not so much handsome as wholesome looking. And he had a way of smiling, she thought, that was just with his eyes. But what she found most appealing of all about him was his way with Danny.

Last night after dinner, C.J. started telling silly knock-knock jokes. Danny laughed so hard that he nearly fell off his chair. She loved watching Danny laugh with abandon. "Don't go. They should be back in just a few minutes. Those boys like their time together in the barn."

"Well, this morning, they've got Jaime out there too."

Mattie was surprised. "I figured she was still sleeping."

"Not Jaime. She's usually up at dawn." C.J. poured himself another cup of coffee. "She likes to take pictures early in the morning. She says the light is best then."

Mattie cracked an egg on the side of a bowl, then another and another. She tried to figure how many more scrambled eggs she should include to feed C.J. and Jaime. It gave her a moment of happiness, a feeling that had been dormant for too long, to have extra mouths to feed. She found she was enjoying having these English guests for Christmas.

"Do you mind if I ask you something personal, Mattie?" C.J. leaned against the counter.

She took out the whisk and started stirring the eggs. "Ask away."

"Have you ever thought about fostering a child?"

The question shocked Mattie. She lost her grip on the bowl and it tilted on its side, so that slippery yolks and whites splattered all over her clean linoleum floor.

C.J. quickly reached for some rags and started to wipe it up. "I'm sorry. Yesterday, in the barn, your husband told me about your miscarriage. I hope . . . I didn't mean to cross a line."

Mattie didn't know what to say. It was sad information, handed to this man within hours of making his acquaintance. But C.J. looked so sorrowful she couldn't help but smile. "Don't apologize. Sounds like Sol told you quite a bit out in the barn." She squeezed out a rag. "More talking goes on in that barn than I would ever imagine."

C.J. leaned back on his heels. "It's just that . . . there's a family at my school who have foster kids. Really great couple. They couldn't have children of their own, but that didn't stop them. They've fostered . . . hmm, I've lost count . . . at least five or six kids. They even adopted two—a brother and a sister. This couple, well, they wanted to be parents and found a way to make it work. And what a difference they've made in the lives of these kids! But if you tell them that, they'd only say that they've been more blessed than the kids. The wife, you kind of remind me of her." Two spots on his cheeks started to flame. "But what do I know? Maybe the Amish don't sponsor foster children?"

"Some do." Mattie took more eggs out of the refrigerator. She wasn't sure what to say, so she didn't say anything.

The truth was, she had brought the topic of adoption up to Sol last summer and was surprised by his strong opposition to the idea. It was the only time they had ever argued. He said he didn't want an outsider's influence in their home.

"But it's a child!" she said. "Hardly an outsider."

Sol didn't see it that way. To him, an invisible wall separated the Amish and the English. He knew the turmoil that came when someone tried to live in both worlds. The wall, Sol insisted, served as protection. It had always been there and it should always remain.

"Seems like fostering is what you're doing with Zach." C.J. stood. "I just meant that it doesn't seem nearly as important to bear a child as it might be to parent a child." He tossed the rags into the sink. "How about if you sit down and let me do the cooking? I know my way around a kitchen."

Mattie was shocked! Every once in a while, Sol would cook something, but only if she wasn't home. C.J. brought her a cup of coffee and pulled out a chair for her. At first, she felt awkward. Imagine sitting in a chair while a man made your breakfast. An English man! Whom she had only known since yesterday! Yet he was very at ease, which made her feel at ease. He was comfortable with himself, with who he was as a man. Unlike his wife, Jaime, who seemed so unsure of herself. Mattie started to relax. It felt rather nice to be waited on.

She listened to him chatter on, this English man in her kitchen, as he cracked eggs with one hand and used the other to slide a slab of butter into a heated cast-iron pan. As the eggs slipped onto the pan, they sizzled. She watched him carefully, worried he would ruin the eggs, but he knew how to cook. Not to cook tidy, though. He was making a big mess and she tried not to cringe as eggshells flew on the floor and dishes piled up in the sink.

He talked as he cooked, telling her that he always wanted to have a big family and he was just waiting for Jaime to feel ready. As he worked, he talked and she listened. He reminded her of her brothers. When they were in the mood, especially when they had a question about girls that perplexed them, they would find Mattie somewhere in the house or the yard, chore alongside her, and just talk and talk. People liked to talk to Mattie about their troubles, she was aware, but she never knew why. She didn't think she had much to offer them other than a listening ear. But she didn't mind listening.

As the sky began to lighten outside, C.J. admitted that he was worried about Jaime. "One of her pictures won a category in a *National Geographic* contest and *boom!*, she hit the radar for her dad—suddenly, he was paying all kinds of attention to her. One weekend, he breezed in like he had just been down to the corner store for a carton of milk. Jaime was thrilled to have him visit. I'd only met him once before—during the wedding—and the wedding was a whole other story—" He rolled his eyes. "That weekend was terrible, just terrible. I was gone on a Search and Rescue. Tucker and I found the victims . . . but it was too late. I was feeling pretty bad about that, and when I finally got home, Jaime and her dad had a surprise for me. They had found a house for us to buy—her dad said he was going to put a down payment on it."

"Why was that such a bad thing?" Mattie asked.

"For one, I'm not really sure he would have ponied up the down payment. He talks big. But even more than that, it seemed his way of undermining me. He doesn't think teaching is a real job."

Mattie's eyebrows went up. "Our elders are trying to pay our teachers more, so that men can raise a family and keep teaching. They think it's that important."

C.J. gave up a wry smile. "Jaime's dad thinks there's only one real job—selling. He's pretty well-to-do—so he says—and he uses his money to impress people." He covered the scrambled eggs with a lid and put the pan into the oven to keep it warm. He flipped over the sizzling bacon in the second frying pan.

"He had also bought a new camera for Jaime that weekend—that very one she was so anxious to get out of the car yesterday. I listened to the two of them trying to convince me to buy this house . . . and I just blew up. Said things I shouldn't have said." He laid the bacon on a paper towel to drain. "I tried to apologize to James later. But he wouldn't accept my apology." He filled a pot with water and set it to boil.

Mattie took a sip of coffee. "Forgiveness works both ways. If you ask for forgiveness from someone, then a person has his own responsibility to accept it."

"Try telling that to her dad. He likes holding power over people." He poured oatmeal into the pot of boiling water. "Seems as if things haven't been the same between Jaime and me since that weekend when her father visited. It's as if she has expectations of me that I can never fulfill." As the oatmeal bubbled up, he started to stir it down. "You know what's funny? I don't think Jaime's pictures with that camera are as good as the ones she took with her old camera. She used to rely on her own eye, on her instincts. It was a film camera. This new one is state-of-the-art digital, with all kinds of bells and whistles. Now she relies on that camera to tell her what a good picture is."

A thought occurred to Mattie. "By any chance, did you give her the old camera?"

He nodded. "It was my wedding gift to her." He shook his head. "I'm sorry to be dumping all of this on you."

Mattie smiled. "My grandfather Caleb used to say, 'Things can get good again. Even things like a marriage.'"

"What if only one of us believes that?"

"Then you wait," Mattie said quietly, stirring a spoonful of sugar into her coffee. "That's what my grandfather would say that we Plain people do best. We wait."

The barn door rumbled shut. Through the window, Mattie could barely make out four bundled figures running toward the house. When they reached the porch, Mattie heard Jaime's musical giggle as she stomped off clumps of snow from her boots. She could see that the sight and sound of her hurt C.J. so much that he flinched.

He turned to Mattie. "What if I'm running out of time?"

Zach drained his juice glass, then spun it absentmindedly on the table. It was the best breakfast he had ever eaten. The English man made them all perfectly cooked scrambled eggs, soft and buttery, topped with sautéed onions and mushrooms and cheese. Zach had wanted to dislike that fellow, the man married to this beautiful creature sitting across the table from him. But he could tell C.J. was a good man. Impossible to dislike, despite his best efforts. He admired the way C.J. treated Jaime—he was kind to her, the way Sol was kind to Mattie. It was one of the things Zach liked about living with Sol and Mattie. He was able to observe, day in and day out, a different kind of marriage than his own folks'. The kind he wanted for himself one day.

It amazed him that the English fellow cooked for everybody. His wife said he cooked most of the time at home. That thought would have baffled his father. He couldn't even imagine his father in a kitchen, other than eating at the table. Nor could he imagine his father treating his mother with kindness.

He glanced over at the mountain of dirty dishes in the kitchen sink. The pale green formica countertops were buried in dishes. The stovetop was splattered with bacon grease and bits of dried-on eggs. C.J. must have used every dish in the house. Ha! That fellow may be able to cook, but he sure couldn't keep a kitchen clean.

He watched Jaime slather jam over her toast. He found himself watching her every move; she was a mystery to him. He was mesmerized by every word she uttered. He had to be careful watching her because he knew that Sol was watching him, but the complexity of her fascinated him. There were so many things he was starting to wonder about her, the loneliness and the restlessness he saw in her.

He finished his eggs and buttered one more piece of toast to go. He was so full he could hardly even sit up, much less bring himself to leave. But the worst of the storm had passed and he wanted to get out to his car to see if he could get it running. Assuming, of course, it wasn't completely buried in a snowdrift. As soon as Sol finished the prayer for breakfast, Zach jumped from the table and plucked his coat and hat off the wall pegs.

"Zach," Sol said, and Zach froze, mid-air. "Before you go fussing over that car of yours, why don't you do Mattie a favor and clean up the breakfast dishes for her?" Sol gave him a cat-in-the-cream smile. "Consider it an early Christmas gift."

The storm was finally losing its bluster. It had taken Zach two hours to clean up the kitchen, including many sighs and moans, but Sol wouldn't let C.J. or anyone else help him. He insisted that Zach wanted to do this for Mattie and ushered everyone into the living room.

C.J. felt a little badly about that—he knew he was a messy cook. At home, he cooked and Jaime cleaned up. It worked for them, though others thought it was a little odd. Jaime's mother had given him an apron for his birthday one year with the saying "I love a man with dishpan hands!"

As soon as Zach finished the last dish, he scowled at Sol and blew out the door to go rescue his car.

In the meantime, Danny peppered C.J. with questions—he wanted to know everything about Search and Rescue, about his Finds, about Tucker, until C.J. felt he had run clean out of stories. Taking pity on C.J., Sol suggested a game of checkers with his son. C.J. envied Mattie and Sol and Danny—not because of their Amish-ness but because of their family-ness: They were smug without meaning to be, smug about the simplest and yet most enduring things in life—their love for each other, their love for their child.

This was how he always sort of imagined it. His life. A cozy day by the hearth, his wife and his children (two sons and two daughters, as long as he was imagining), a big dog like Tucker curled up in front of the fire. Everyone content, just being together.

When they had finished breakfast this morning, Sol prayed aloud a prayer that was profound in its simplicity: "The days available to say a kind word to someone this year are rapidly drawing to a close. Lord God, teach us to be kind."

That's the word he would use to tell Eve what the Amish were like: kind. They have a culture of kindness. He and Eve played a game called One Word they invented during a rainy lunch in the teacher's lounge. She had asked him to describe his work, his mother, his father, his dog, his wife—each one in a single word. Eve used words like *philology* and *pedantic* without batting an eye. So he had spent time finding just the right word to impress her. In the end, he said *unpredictable* (work), *mother wit* (mother), *trustworthy* (father), *loyal* (Tucker).

"And your wife?" Eve had asked. "How would you describe her?"

He took a long time with that one. *Charming*, he considered. *Cute. Talented. Funny. Insecure. Enthralling. Independent.* Which one word best described Jaime? Then, suddenly, he knew.

"Asymmetrical."

C.J. looked across the room at his wife. Mattie was trying to teach Jaime how to sew a straight stitch. Their two heads were bowed over the frame. The sight made him smile. He doubted Jaime had ever threaded a needle in her life. She looked so relaxed, so at ease. She had showered after breakfast and her hair hung loose and curly, the way it naturally was before she started her Anti-Curl Program. Her hair was finally growing longer.

He had been horrified when she surprised him with that bizarre haircut—clipped short on one side, but jaw-length and jagged on the other. They had a terrible fight over it—their worst ever. She cried when she saw how disappointed he was in the haircut. Everyone in New York City was wearing their hair this way, she insisted. Why would *that* matter? he pointed out, when we live in Stoney Ridge? Then he asked, under his breath but a little too loudly, when was she ever going to stop reinventing herself?

"When I finally get it right!" she shouted and stomped away.

This morning, she wasn't wearing any makeup. Her shirt wasn't tucked in; it hung over her pants. She looked . . . the way she used to look before James MacComber entered the scene and took her to get an expensive makeover. Before she became Asymmetrical Haircut Jaime. That blasted haircut had become a metaphor for how she had changed this last year. Out of balance.

C.J. had always thought Jaime was a beauty—a natural outdoor beauty. No makeup, no hairspray. She smelled like a pinecone. But lately she looked like an exquisite china doll, delicate, fragile, but a little hard and stiff, just like the hairspray she lacquered on her hair to keep every strand in place. Jaime liked her new look, but he missed the old Jaime. Now she was constantly worried about money and clothes and a house and new cars and money again. He missed the Jaime who used to love his jeep, loved to hike in the woods, loved Tucker. The Jaime who loved him.

The woodstove kept the room warm and toasty, and for a moment, C.J. wished the storm would just continue raging. He glanced out the window and saw some blue behind some clouds, and he actually felt disappointed. Suddenly this Christmas weekend felt short and precious; he wanted it to last forever.

The thought of leaving this cozy room to go on a cruise with James MacComber made C.J. feel ill, as if he were being smothered. A cruise meant he would be trapped with nowhere to go but to listen to Jaime's father pontificate about his latest sales deal. Her father was mysteriously wealthy. C.J. could never quite figure how or what he did for a living—he wheeled and dealed and dabbled in all kinds of things. He loved to name-drop too—famous people he had met (the truth of which C.J. had somehow always doubted), or designer this or that, or had C.J. seen this latest technology? and he would whip out some new gadget. He did not trust James MacComber. Never had.

The first time he met Jaime's father was the day before their wedding, when he suddenly arrived and acted like he was footing the bill for the entire wedding. He told Jaime he wanted to walk her down the aisle—and Jaime let him! Then he didn't think that a buffet meal for the reception was ritzy enough, so he canceled the buffet C.J. and Jaime had chosen and substituted a sit-down dinner menu, including lobster tails for everyone. Lobster tails. In Pennsylvania, in late December. Although he had made a big show of acting like a host at the reception, he never did end up paying for anything. Jaime's mother didn't have the money to pay for a sit-down dinner, so C.J. sold his motorcycle to pay off the restaurant bill. How he had loved that motorcycle! Thus ended his first experience with James MacComber's style of fatherhood.

But C.J. had agreed to go on this cruise and he would go, for Jaime's sake. By noon, the sky was empty of clouds, bright blue, and the winter sun reflected off the snow so brightly that it hurt to gaze outside the windows too long. C.J. saw something on the road and shaded his eyes to look as the object turned into Sol and Mattie's drive. It was a horse-drawn sleigh, led by an enormous horse, carrying three Amish men.

Sol came up behind him. "Well, look at that. Our neighbors are here to help get that car out of the pond." He reached for his hat and jacket off the wall peg.

C.J. grabbed his jacket too. "But how could they possibly have known? With a doozy of a storm like that, how could they have known?"

Sol grinned. "One farmer probably passed by and saw it, told another, then another. It's called the Amish telegraph system."

Jaime came into the kitchen. "Do you think they can get the car out of the pond without a tow truck?"

"Looks like we're going to give it a try," Sol said. "But we're sure to need another horse. I'll go get Dixie."

Danny pulled on his boots and coat and mittens as Sol spoke to Jaime.

Mattie stood against the doorjamb between the kitchen and the living room. Her arms were folded against her chest. "Sol, that's dangerous work. I don't know that Danny should be down there."

"Oh Mom!" Danny whined.

"Mattie," Sol said in a sharp voice. "The boy needs to learn how to do things like this. You can't keep him in the kitchen for the rest of his life."

C.J. saw Mattie glance from Jaime to him, then turn her head away, embarrassed. She lifted her head and drew her shoulders up proud. It was her quiet way, C.J. thought, of making her stand. Stubborn but silent. He held back a smile. It relieved him to see that even a couple like Mattie and Sol had their tense moments.

"I'll keep a close watch on him," Sol said in a softer tone. He touched Mattie's arm and they exchanged a long look, connected for a moment in a way that excluded everyone else.

C.J. watched with a rush of longing. He and Jaime used to have those kinds of looks—filled with silent communication.

Maybe Mattie's grandfather was right. Maybe things could get good again.

Mattie's light spirits from the pleasant morning had fizzled away. She watched Sol lead Dixie, their buggy horse, out of the barn and down toward the pond. Danny followed close behind, holding a coil of rope. The English visitors trailed behind both of them, following in the path cleared by Dixie's large hoofprints. That big dog, Tucker, didn't need a path. He was jumping around for joy in the snowdrifts.

She felt a pull on her heart as she watched Danny trudge down the hill. She hoped Sol would truly pay close attention to him. Even though the pond was probably frozen solid from last night's freezing temperatures, pulling the car out would break up the ice. Danny had just learned to swim last August and he wasn't very good at it. She wondered if she should go down with them, but she knew Sol would know why she was there, that she didn't trust him to watch over their son.

She wondered how long pulling the car out would take, and if the neighbors would be expecting lunch. Just the thought of making lunch for all of them made her feel tired. She was always so tired lately, worn down by worries and what-ifs. She knew it wasn't right, but she couldn't seem to keep her mind from racing. She rubbed her face.

What is happening to me? I'm turning into someone I never wanted to be. She thought of the dark feelings, foreign feelings, that filled her when she was at Carrie Miller's last weekend. She held Carrie's beautiful newborn daughter in her arms—oh, how she wished she were hers! She hugged the baby close to her, breathing in her baby smell. The baby was even named Mathilda after Mattie—and yet she felt something close to bitterness toward Carrie—*a woman who is like a sister to me.* Bitterness that felt like bile in her throat. It disgusted Mattie to admit those feelings to herself.

But why couldn't it be she who had a baby? Why was it that her sisters-in-law and friends could do something that she couldn't seem to do? Carrie and Abel had three children now; some of her friends had even more!

Mattie had grown up wanting thirteen children. A baker's dozen, her mother had called it. She remembered the early years of her marriage, remembered lying in Sol's arms and whispering dreams of all the babies they would make together. They even had names picked out. But the nights had passed into months, and the months into years. *I've got to surrender this deep longing, but I just can't seem to let it go. Dear God, when I am weak, you are strong.* Tears blurred her eyes and filled her throat. She had to swallow twice to fight them back. She would not cry!

As she turned to go upstairs, she noticed Jaime's camera on the table. She stopped and picked it up. It was a complicated piece of equipment, covered with precise dials and levers. She set it down again, fearful she would break it. Then she rolled her eyes. *I'm even afraid of a silly thing like a camera.*

Zach shifted his weight from foot to foot, trying to keep from freezing. The wind had a stiff bite to it, and even though the sky was blue and clear, there was talk that another storm was heading in. Standing next to him and Sol were three other men, discussing the best way to get the English visitors' car out of the pond. He was sure that if these neighbors knew of the stuck car, his father did too. But, of course, his father was too righteous to help anyone with car trouble.

He didn't know why this endeavor took so much discussion. Seemed to him all they needed to do was to get rope, horses, and start to pull. But the ice worried the older men. He wasn't sure why *they* were so worried. He knew they would be sending him to wade into that pond to tie the rope to the bumper. At least he was wearing his fishing boots today.

He wasn't terribly eager to have the car pulled out of the pond. That meant Jaime Fitzpatrick would be on her way, out of his life forever. It was wrong to have such thoughts about an English woman, a *married* English woman, but Jaime was different than any woman he had ever met. He looked over at her and saw how impatient she was to get her car out of the pond. She was stretching up and down on her toes, her arms folded tightly against her chest. He could practically see her biting her tongue to keep from telling the men to get going. Get that car—that sleek, stunning piece of machinery—out of the pond!

Who could blame her? What kind of a woman had a sports car like that, anyway? Owning such a vehicle was one more thing about Jaime that fascinated him. Sol elbowed him, and when Zach looked to see what he wanted, he saw the warning scowl on Sol's face.

Zach felt his cheeks start to flush. Oh, surely, nothing good could come from such wicked thoughts.

If Sol weren't standing next to the three most humorless men in his church, he would have picked up Zach by the scruff of his neck and thrown him in the pond to cool off his ardor. That ridiculous look of adoration on Zach's face as he gawked at the English woman was the last straw. What thoughts ran through that boy's head? None with any sense, that's for sure.

When Zach first came to live with them, Sol saw him as the lovable screw-up of the family. He and Mattie would shake their heads at his antics in fond disbelief. But Zach's self-absorbed behavior soon grew tiresome—late nights, careless work habits, his immature friends. The gall to hide a car on Sol's farm. And now, he'd developed a schoolboy crush on a married English woman. *Married!* Enough! Sol had *had it* with that boy. It was time for Zach to move on.

Mattie would not like his decision. He could practically hear her objections: "Is that what you're going to do with our own Danny when it's time for him to try out his wings? Cut him off? Pretend he doesn't exist? But you know as well as anybody, Solomon Riehl"—she only called him Solomon when she wanted to make a point—"God doesn't write *anybody* off."

He did know that. He was a church member today because Mattie didn't write him off. She kept seeing the potential of manhood within him, even when he wasn't sure it was there himself. But she also wasn't aware of the pressure he was getting from church members, from Zach's own father, to allow the boy to face up to his own consequences.

"He'll never learn," Eli Zook told him at church two weeks ago, pointing a long bony finger at Sol's chest, "if you and Mattie keep sheltering him. You're only hobbling the boy with kindness."

It looked like the three men were finally coming to a consensus about how to get the car out of the pond. That meant the English visitors could be on their way. He felt a tiny twinge of sorrow about that. It surprised him to have such a thought cross his mind, but these visitors had been good for Mattie. He saw the sadness leave her face this morning during breakfast, a sadness that had covered her lately like a blanket. She even laughed a few times. She used to laugh so often. It pleased him to see her enjoying herself. Life could be funny like that, Sol thought. *Here I thought we were helping those English guests out, when the truth was they were helping us.*

Sol had encouraged Mattie to believe the doctor's words, that there was plenty of time for more children, that God would bless them still. But Sol knew life wasn't turning out the way they planned. Not having more children was a source of great grief to him and it was a hard thing to accept. He scolded Mattie for overprotecting Danny, but the truth was, he was just as guilty of it. Maybe not trying to keep him from every possible physical danger, the way Mattie did, but he was terrified of losing Danny to the world.

He glanced at Zach. *That* was the real reason he wanted to send Zach on his way—back to his parents or out to the world. This weekend, his worry about Zach's sway over Danny spiked to a new level; he felt he had to do something . . . soon. Danny was far more observant of Zach than Sol had realized. He had ferreted out that car. And it was the first time Danny had kept something secret from his father.

Nip it now, Sol thought, as he followed the men down to the pond. *Nip it in the bud.*

It was fascinating, C.J. thought, to see how the Amish improvised. They got things done quite efficiently without the benefit of a motor. The harnesses of two deluxe-sized horses, with legs thicker than tree trunks, were attached to a plow, which was attached by ropes to the bumper of Jaime's car. Little by little, the horses eased the car out of the frozen pond, breaking up the ice. Jaime jumped up and down like a schoolgirl when the back wheels of the car rose out of the shards of ice and murky water. Sol kept the horses moving forward, pulling and straining, until they reached flat ground. C.J. thought he would never forget the sound of horses' hooves sucking and plopping in the banks of the pond. It was a miracle! Without any modern intervention. He had figured it might be February before that car could be budged.

Not that he cared. He hated that car. Jaime's father had given it to her for her birthday in October—it was waiting outside of their apartment with a gigantic ribbon on it and included one of those horrible vanity plates: My #1 Girl. Jaime burst into happy tears when she discovered it was from her father.

Then, one week later, came the real surprise. The first monthly leasing bill, forty-eight to follow, the contract said. He called James to ask him about it and James just laughed it off. "Oh, must be a billing mistake. I'll take care of it."

Then the bill for November came. Then December.

C.J. talked it over with Eve and she suggested returning the car to the dealer, but that would mean he would have to tell Jaime the slippery trick her father had done. He just couldn't do it. She had been so pleased with the attention her father was showing her. He knew the toll her mother's death had taken on her. Tolerating this car seemed like a small way to lessen that pain, so instead, he quietly paid the bills with money they didn't have to spare.

Sol gave C.J. the go-ahead to get inside the car and set the emergency brake before he unhooked the horses. At first, the car's door handle was frozen, but one of the Amish neighbors gently pushed C.J. aside and cupped his mouth around the lock. He blew and blew on it, then pulled it again.

"Bingo!" the Amish man said, revealing missing molars in his large grin.

C.J. jumped into the driver's seat, turned over the ignition once, then twice, and the engine caught! He looked at Jaime and gave her a thumbs-up, grinning when he saw the delighted look on her face.

As Jaime saw her car emerge out of the water—her beautiful new car—she felt almost giddy with happiness. She hoped that the sleigh might pack down the snow hard enough that they could follow behind it until they reached the main road. Surely, the roads would be cleared by snowplows soon. She felt a bloom of optimism from the thought and let out a deep, relieved sigh. They would be able to meet her father today in time to leave for the trip. Everything was back on track.

She saw C.J. talking to the Amish farmers, then he went back to the car and reached in to get her purse. He brought it to her.

"They're debating what to do next." He looked back at the group of bearded men, huddling together in a circle, listening carefully to each other. "They seem to feel a consensus is important before they take the next step."

Jaime laughed. "Aren't they wonderful to us, C.J.? One

way or another, we're going to make it on the cruise ship tomorrow. It's a miracle!"

C.J. rolled his eyes. "Oh sure. I can't think of anything more pressing on God's agenda on this Christmas Eve than making sure we get on that cruise."

While he kept his gaze on the group of farmers, Jaime took a step back. Then another. She stopped and scooped up a handful of snow, packing it into a ball. She heaved the snowball at C.J.'s head but missed and hit his back instead. He turned toward her with a startled look on his face. She bent over to gather more snow, straightened up, and fired a snowball that hit him on his chin. He looked at her, stunned, then broke into a smile. Slowly, he bent down and picked up some snow, then packed it into a hard ball.

He took a step toward her; she whirled to run, but the snow made her clumsy and she fell. C.J.'s snowball landed gently on the top of her head, making her shudder as the snow went down inside the open collar of her coat. She spat snow out of her mouth, shook it off her eyelashes and her hair. He came over to help her get up and she put her hands up to grab his, then released him so he fell down too. They looked at each other, and Jaime started to smile, then to laugh at the sight of C.J., toppled over. He started laughing too, and the two of them sat there, ridiculously, in the snow like a couple of kids, laughing so hard that tears rolled down their cheeks.

When had they last laughed like that? She couldn't remember. But it felt so good.

C.J. reached over and gently brushed snow off Jaime's face. His gaze fastened on her mouth. His hand stole up to frame her cheek, his thumb stroking the line of her jaw. Their breath entwined like white wedding ribbons in the air. As he lowered his head to kiss her, he caught sight of five Amish farmers and Danny, staring at the two of them sitting in the snow like a couple of kids.

He froze.

In the silence of that moment, he heard a strange ringing sound. The Amish men, including Danny, turned their heads in the direction of the sound. Could that possibly be . . . a cell phone? How could a cell phone have a signal out here in the middle of nowhere? It was coming from Jaime's purse.

C.J. scrambled to his feet and grabbed her purse to toss to her. "I think your cell is ringing."

He brushed the snow off his jacket and pants, shivering as he felt some snow slip down his back. He thought about trying to get into the car's trunk to see if water had seeped in. He felt a tap on his shoulder and turned toward Jaime. She handed him the cell phone with a strange, hard look on her face.

"It's for you," Jaime said coldly. "It's Eve."

Eve? How did she get Jaime's cell phone number? "Hello?" he said warily.

"C.J.!" Eve said. "I'm so glad I caught you before you left on the cruise! Guess what?"

C.J. watched Jaime watching him. She looked steamed. "Um, Eve, I'm in a little bit of a predicament here. How did you get this number?"

"It's your emergency number, for work. And this is an emergency!"

"What's wrong?" He turned away from Jaime's stare and lowered his voice. "Are you all right? Has something happened?"

"Yes, something has happened! You've been chosen as the

district's Teacher of the Year! You won, C.J! That means that now you're a finalist for regionals, then state! Al found out yesterday and he would have called you himself, but he had that big family get-together, so he asked me to call you, and you don't carry a cell phone so I had to find another way to reach you." She finally took a breath. "You don't mind, do you? Am I interrupting anything important?"

C.J. was stunned. He had been pleased his principal, Al, had wanted to nominate him for the award—Eve had spent hours helping to fill out the application this fall. He never dreamed he would win. Never! He was so sure he wouldn't win that he didn't even tell Jaime about it. He didn't want her telling her father about it, only to have to face him if he lost. To C.J., getting nominated was enough.

Before he could even react, a click came through on call waiting. "Eve, that's great news. Really great! Thanks for letting me know. I'll get back to you. Merry Christmas!" He pressed the call waiting button. "Hello?"

Oh. Jaime's father. He said a brief hello to James and handed the phone to Jaime. He turned back to see if the Amish farmers had decided if they were going to tow the car to the road or not. For a moment, though, he stood right where he was, letting Eve's news sink in. *Teacher of the Year! Me?!*

Danny came up to him and pulled on his jacket sleeve to get his attention. He pointed a small finger toward Jaime, so C.J. spun around to face her.

Jaime had the receiver pressed against her ear. "Dad, the snowstorm kind of derailed us—it's a long story, but I'll fill you in later. We can still make it. There's even time to meet the agent." As she listened to her father, C.J. saw the enthusiasm drain from her face. "What does that mean? What do you mean, 'some other time'? Why?" Her face went from looking worried to shocked. Then, horrified. "You're getting *married*? Married? *That's* the big surprise you had for me?" An expression of panic crossed over her as she listened. "Dad, why can't you just wait? The car just got pulled—" She looked at C.J., dazed. "He hung up."

C.J. forgot about the car and the Amish men and the Teacher of the Year recognition. He took a few steps closer to her. Her gaze was fixed on the phone she held in her hands.

"He's at the airport," she said quietly. "He and . . . Sheila, I think he said her name was. They're leaving now, to beat the next storm. They're getting married on the cruise. That's his big surprise. Getting married. He's leaving without me."

She covered her face with her hands. Then she started to cry in a way that he had only seen her cry once or twice before—slowly at first, then louder and louder, shaking and sobbing. C.J. wrapped her up in his arms and held her, patting her back to console her.

At first, the bewildered look on the Amish men's faces as they observed Jaime's meltdown almost made C.J. laugh. It shouldn't have struck him as funny, but it did. The somber worry on their kind, bearded faces, trying to help pry a car out of a frozen pond—when the Amish didn't even drive cars.

C.J. saw Sol lift his shoulders helplessly and C.J. gave him the OK signal with his fingers. Sol turned and spoke to the others. It looked like they had come to a decision. They were going to drag the car down to the end of the lane, so it would be ready to go when the snowplows came through, he assumed. They seemed relieved to be doing something, talking to each other in their language. They must think that he and Jaime were . . . crazy. Crazy English people. Here she was, crying as if her heart was breaking. He didn't blame them for being confused by Jaime's weeping. How could he explain

Jaime's father to these gentle people? He hardly understood James MacComber himself.

What kind of father ignores his daughter most of her life? Then suddenly decides she's worth paying attention to, after all. The kind of attention James paid usually left Jaime feeling conflicted and upset . . . about herself, about her work, about him.

And now James is getting married. It figured! What was this, wife number five?

It was good that his thoughts were hidden, C.J. realized. They were running along the lines of being delighted that the cruise was off. Overjoyed! And behind that was a deep-down lingering happiness that started when Jaime threw a snowball at him. They hadn't had fun together in such a long time. He couldn't even remember the last time they shared a laugh, the way they used to. How he missed her! He had lost her six months ago, when he wasn't watching, and although it wasn't his fault entirely, he didn't want to lose her again.

Danny came up beside C.J. and whispered, "I have an idea to help. Can I take Tucker with me?"

C.J. nodded and Danny turned and ran up toward the house, with Tucker following close behind.

After the car was towed to the end of the long driveway, Sol helped his neighbors hook the sleigh traces back to the horse's harness and waved goodbye as they disappeared down the street. He led Dixie into her stall and gave her a few handfuls of oats as a thank-you for helping pull that car out of the pond. Dixie mouthed Sol's hands with her big lips, scattering oats over the ground. He made sure the water bucket was full, then checked the rest of the stock in the barn, as he always did. His last stop was with the ewe and lamb. He paused for a moment. A ray of sun beamed through the upper barn window and shone down on the pair, sleeping in a corner. It felt holy, that moment.

He lingered awhile longer, hoping the English woman was done with her wailing. At first, he thought someone had died, she was *that* overcome. But then he heard she was upset because her father left on that boat trip. It seemed odd to him that the father wouldn't wait. He knew if his own father were in that spot, he would rather give up a trip than give up time with his family. He didn't know if that was what set her off, but he was happy to get away from it.

Sol felt a little sorry for the English husband. He and Mattie were no strangers to sorrow, but he could never imagine her carrying on the way that English woman did.

Mattie! Suddenly he realized that he didn't know where Danny was.

He picked up his hat and fit it snug. Just as he reached out to slide open the barn door, Zach beat him to it, carrying a large bundle of rope over his shoulder. Zach nodded at him and walked past him to hang the rope on the wall.

Sol kept a hand on the open door, looked back at Zach, let out a sigh, and closed the door shut. "Zach, let's talk for a moment."

A dull ache had spread through Jaime's chest as her father's intent became clear on the phone. She felt as if she had been hit by a tidal wave of grief, of longing.

Why did her father have that effect on her? More important,

why did she let him? She pulled back from C.J. and wiped her face with her gloves. "I'm sorry, C.J. I wish I knew what was wrong with me. I'm such a mess."

"Maybe it would be good to talk to someone."

"Oh great. You mean, a shrink? You think I'm a mess too." She crossed her arms against her chest.

"No, I don't think you're a mess. And I didn't mean a shrink. Maybe, like a pastor. Or better still, God."

She stepped back from him. Lately, things always circled back to church for C.J. They belonged to the Presbyterian church in Lancaster that they had been married in, but they had never been strict about attending. Jaime was certain God existed, but she wasn't quite as certain that God knew she existed. She had never had much use for faith—not the way her mother relied on her faith, or C.J. was starting to rely on his—and the day her mother was killed, Jaime found her spiritual reserve empty. There was nothing to draw on.

"On the phone to your dad, you said something about meeting an agent." C.J. looked at her suspiciously. "What was that about? What has your father promised you now?"

There was a pause. One beat. Then two. She was cornered. She had planned to tell C.J. about the photography agent friend of her father's while they were driving to her father's. Not now. Not like this.

C.J. took a step closer to Jaime. "Listen to me. Your father is all talk. No action."

"My father has been incredibly generous to us!" She pointed to the car. "He bought me that car! He bought me the camera. He sends me flowers! He takes me shopping!"

"You're defending him? Today? Just as he's getting married to wife number twelve—"

"Four!"

"Five! And he's leaving without you on a cruise that he had promised to take you on, to help you get through this first Christmas without your mother—"

"It's not his fault that the storm has interfered! At least he's trying! He wanted me there for his wedding to Shelley."

"Sheila."

"Whatever! The point is, he wants us to join him. He said he would buy our plane tickets if we were able to join them."

"What?" C.J. roared. "I thought he had offered to pay for our trip! Do you mean that we were going to have to pay for it ourselves?" He was livid. "Money! It always boils down to your dad and his money."

"That's his way of making up for all those years of being absent! He's showing his love!"

"Love? This is his way of throwing his weight around! And he always waits until he has an audience, then he pulls out his wallet and gives you his Visa. Or hundred dollar bills."

"You're just jealous of his success!" She knew she sounded childish, but she was upset and angry and . . . so *very* disappointed. Her father had given her the impression that her Christmas surprise was going to be setting her up with a New York photography agent. He had practically promised! This was going to be the way she would finally connect to him, to finally have him in her life. She was willing to completely uproot her life to be near him. And this cruise was going to patch up her marriage! It was going to be the answer they needed. Time away from Stoney Ridge, from sad memories, from that harridan, Eve. She was sure she could convince C.J. that they needed to make this move. It would launch her photography career. She would finally start making some money. Big money, real money, her dad had said. And C.J. could find a teaching job anywhere!

Instead, her father was getting married, to some Sherry-bimbo that he probably met last month. All of Jaime's plans, her hopes—they were all disappearing, like wisps of steam from a cup of tea.

C.J. threw his hands in the air. "What are you talking about? I have never wanted that kind of success. Success for me is having a job with meaning. It's having relationships that endure!"

Like the enduring relationship with Eve?! she wanted to shout, but she refused to say it out loud. She wasn't going to make this easy for him. He was the one who was dallying with someone else. Not her. "And that job means we'll be living in an apartment for the rest of our life."

"It might mean we don't have the kind of house your father thinks you should have, but we'll have a house, in due time."

She threw up her hands. "When, C.J.? And how are we ever going to be able to buy a house on a teacher's salary?"

He crossed his arms against his chest. "You knew what my life was like when you married me."

But did I? Did anybody really know what married life would be like? "You don't understand—"

"What? What *don't* I understand? That you seem to feel entitled to things, because that's how your father shows you affection? That's not love, Jaime. He might be your father, but he's never been your dad. Dads stick around. Dads don't disappear and only show up when their child wins a contest." His face was flushed, and his voice was strong, filling the air around them, demanding an answer.

They stared at each other for a long time, until an odd grinding sound floated across the hillside. It was a snowplow, slowly making its way along the road in front of the farmhouse.

Jaime turned to C.J. with a delighted look on her face. "The trip! Maybe we could still make it!"

She saw Sol and Zach cross from the barn to the house and ran to meet them, to tell them that they would be leaving. It wasn't until she almost reached the farmhouse that she looked back and saw C.J. was still standing there, by the pond's edge, where she had left him.

───────────※───────────

Mattie woke from a nap, startled by the rumble of voices below her bedroom window. It took her a moment to gather her thoughts, and as soon as she did, she jumped out of bed and hurried to the window. She saw that Jaime's red car was no longer in the pond, but now it was down at the edge of the driveway. The hood was up and she could see Zach, bent over, examining the engine. There was no sign of their neighbors. Land sakes, how long had she slept? She just meant to lie down on the bed for a moment. As she smoothed her hair under her prayer cap, she realized it was Sol's deep voice that woke her. He was below their bedroom window, talking to Jaime on the porch.

She pinned her black apron back over her teal-colored dress and tied her sneaker laces. Before she reached the bottom of the stairs, Jaime and Sol came through the kitchen door. When Jaime saw her, she rushed to meet her.

"Mattie! It's a miracle! The car is down by the lane and the snowplow just came through. We're able to get back on schedule!" As Jaime gave Mattie a blow-by-blow account of the last hour, C.J. opened the door to join them in the kitchen.

Mattie took in Jaime's excitement; she noticed C.J. didn't look quite as excited. Then she turned to Sol. "Where's Danny?"

An unnatural silence fell over the room as Sol, C.J., and Jaime exchanged puzzled looks.

"I thought he went up to the house with Tucker," C.J. said. "Awhile ago."

Mattie felt as if the strange quiet were expanding from someplace in the center of her, rippling through the kitchen.

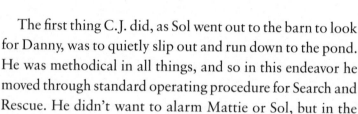

The first thing C.J. did, as Sol went out to the barn to look for Danny, was to quietly slip out and run down to the pond. He was methodical in all things, and so in this endeavor he moved through standard operating procedure for Search and Rescue. He didn't want to alarm Mattie or Sol, but in the confusion of the moment, he knew that the pond had to be ruled out first.

It relieved him that Tucker was with Danny. He whistled for Tucker, scanning the pond for any sign of the boy or the dog. He started to try to catalog details about Danny: the clothes he was wearing, what kind of boots he had on, whether the weight of his clothes would cause him to sink. He knew Tucker wouldn't leave Danny, but it crossed his mind that they both could have drowned in the frigid temperatures, quickly and quietly.

How long ago had he seen Danny? He thought of Danny coming up to him, telling him that he wanted to borrow Tucker, right after Jaime got off the phone with her father. How long ago was that? He guessed it was twenty minutes, at least. Maybe longer.

He walked along the edge of the pond until he was satisfied that there was no sign of them. No tracks. No disturbance of the ice other than where the car was ripped out. He took a large stick and pushed the ice around where the car had been, until he was thoroughly satisfied. He threw the stick down and started looking around the yard to see if there were any fresh tracks. Every few minutes, he whistled for Tucker, then listened carefully for a bark in return.

Nothing.

If Tucker heard his whistle, he wouldn't ignore it. He saw Sol cross from the barn to the house, no sign of Danny and Tucker. Concern started to spike inside of C.J. He looked up at the sky. The clear blue of an hour ago was beginning to change. Some gray clouds were starting to gather in the north—a portent of that second storm.

Jaime met him halfway down the lane. "Mattie and I have looked all through the house. Where could he be?"

C.J. blew air out of his mouth. "He's a bright boy. He knows this farm."

She glanced at the pond. "Did you think he was down there?"

"I just wanted to make sure. There was so much going on. He could have slipped and fallen in without anyone seeing."

"Tucker would have barked."

C.J. nodded.

"Mattie's terribly worried."

C.J. started back up to the house. "Little boys wander off all the time. I'm sure he'll be back soon."

She hurried to catch up to him. "So then, maybe . . . do you think . . . maybe we could leave pretty soon?"

C.J. stopped in his tracks. "With Danny missing? With Tucker gone?"

She studied her feet. "If you feel they're not in any trouble, don't you think it would be okay to leave? We could come back and get Tucker when we get back. I'm sure they wouldn't mind watching him for the week. We could pay them, instead of the kennel." She lifted her head, a pleading look on her face. "I wouldn't ask if it weren't so important."

C.J. looked at his wife, stunned. When C.J. first met Jaime, he knew this was the girl he'd been waiting for. He'd always thought love at first sight was a tired cliché, but that's what happened to him. It was like getting hit in the gut, a right cross to the chin. She was funny, fascinating, quirky, ridiculously insecure. Beautiful—and completely indifferent to it. He knew she was young, a little immature, with some lingering issues from her father's abandonment. Even more issues since James had shown back up—and what was the deal with James promising to set her up with a big-time agent? He'd overheard enough of their conversation to know he'd eventually have to clean up that mess too. Why couldn't her father behave like a father instead of a manager?

But not a day had gone by that C.J. hadn't looked at Jaime with love in his heart. Right now, though—at this very moment—he didn't like this person who stood before him. "You go ahead and go, if it's that important to you. But I'm not leaving. Not until I know Danny is safe." He started back up to the house.

"C.J., I'm not meaning to sound heartless," she called out. "You said yourself that Danny will be back soon."

C.J. didn't stop walking, even as Jaime caught up with him. "I'm not going to leave until Danny and Tucker are home, safe and sound." With a grand sweep of his hand, he added, "But *you* are free to go."

Mattie rushed upstairs from the basement when she heard Sol's footsteps in the kitchen. When Danny was four, he had gone missing and she had found him down in the basement. He had gone down to sample the deer jerky that had just come out of the smoker and fell sound asleep.

"Was he in the barn?"

Sol shook his head.

"Did you look everywhere? The hayloft? You know how he likes to play up there. Could he have fallen?"

"I looked every place in the barn that I could think of."

Mattie held on to the counter to steady herself. She felt as if the world had become very fragile. At any given moment, anything at all could happen. "I have a terrible feeling inside, Sol. I can't explain it. Something is wrong."

Sol put his hands on her shoulders. "Mattie, you think something terrible is going to happen every blessed day. You've been thinking that way for a long time now."

She buried her face in his shoulder. "I know. But this feels different."

Sol squeezed her tightly against him. "You have to get ahold of yourself and let him be a normal boy, Mattie. Knowing Danny, he probably wandered off for a hike in the woods with the dog. It's good he has that dog with him too."

She pulled back. "Why? Why is that good?"

"Because he's not alone. That English dog won't leave him."

Mattie felt her fear lighten a little, but she couldn't let go of a foreboding. Was it just her mind playing tricks on her? "Didn't you say another storm was coming in? Right on the heels of this one, you said so yourself, at breakfast." She looked over at the windows in the living room at the sky. A few gray clouds were sailing across the blue.

"He's fine. He'll be back long before then."

"You don't know that, Sol. Just by saying something doesn't

make it so. You can't fix everything! People are not machines, like a table saw that just needs a new part. You can't give out new parts!"

Sol looked confused. "Are we talking about Danny?"

"Yes! No! I don't know." She sniffed and wiped her cheeks with her hands.

"He'll be back soon, safe and sound." He put his arms around her and pulled her close to his body. "I don't want you to fret about this."

But both of them knew she would.

Jaime watched C.J. walk into the farmhouse kitchen. She couldn't believe he told her she could leave without him! Those words pierced her. Jaime was sure he would insist on going with her. Didn't he want to go with her? Did he mean it? Would he really let her leave without him?

She glanced back at the car. The snowplow was coming the other way now, clearing off the side of the road that led to Mattie and Sol's driveway. She *could* leave now. She could make it to the airport and catch an afternoon flight to Miami. Maybe she should call C.J.'s bluff. He was always so hard on her father. He never tried to see things from her father's viewpoint. Maybe her father was just trying to hide his disappointment that they weren't able to make the trip. Maybe the tickets were nonrefundable and her father was just too thoughtful to say so. It might be easier to take that trip without C.J. Maybe they both needed time apart, to think. But what would it mean to them if she left now? She rubbed her face with her gloves. Why did it feel as if he had left her?

She felt the sting of C.J.'s words, that she thought she was entitled to things. He wasn't wrong. She did want more. Was it so wrong to want a house and a car and nice things to go along with it? Or what about wanting a husband who didn't get phone calls from a woman named Eve? She looked up at the farmhouse. It was so simple and plain. There was nothing fancy about this Amish home, cheerful and bustling with activity. They may not have much, but they had love. What would her father say about a house like this? Not long ago, he told Jaime he had the Italian marble torn out of a bathroom because he didn't quite like the color. What would Mattie and Sol think of that?

Then an odd thought crossed her mind. Her father's home was empty. And lonely. And now he was going on his fifth marriage.

She noticed Mattie looking out the kitchen window as Sol came up behind her, putting an arm protectively around her shoulders. C.J. stood nearby. Could Danny really be in trouble? Boys wandered off all the time, C.J. had said so himself.

Stop me! she wanted to shout to C.J. *Come and get me! Don't let me leave!* As it was, she was going to have to take this step of her own free will. The decision was hers.

Jaime turned and walked down to her car. Zach had the hood up and was hovering over the engine like a surgeon puzzling over his patient in an operating room. "Zach, have you seen Danny? Or Tucker?"

Zach shook his hands at his sides, loosely, as if to release leftover energy. "Not for a little while."

"Think it's true that another storm is coming in?" She scanned the clear blue sky for clouds but didn't see any.

Zach shrugged. "Maybe."

"Mattie thinks he's gone missing."

Zach scratched his head. "Mattie . . . she tends to be a little . . ." He made a clockwise motion with his hand. "She tends to worry a lot. But then, I might worry about a boy like Danny too."

"Does he go missing very much?"

"Danny's always getting into something or other. He's six . . . and he's just . . . Danny."

Jaime's gaze shifted up toward the house, then back to her car.

"You leaving soon?" he asked.

She let out a soughing sound. "I think so."

"Would you mind dropping me off in town on your way out?"

"Where are you headed on Christmas Eve?"

Zach looked away. "I'm leaving. Sol told me that it's time I make it on my own. The car was the last straw. He wants me to leave." He thrust his hands to the bottoms of his pockets and hunched up as if he were in a hailstorm. "Says he thinks I'm a bad influence on Danny."

"Are you?"

He wiggled his eyebrows in that way that made her laugh. "Sometimes." He took a step closer to her and lowered his voice. "Have you ever seen an ocean?"

She nodded. "Sure. A bunch of times. My mom and I used to go to the Jersey shore for a week each summer."

"What's it like?"

"The ocean?" She smiled. "The biggest thing you ever could imagine. Water that stretches as far as your eye can see, until it slips off the horizon. And every day is different. The water changes color! Sometimes, the ocean is a glassy sea, a shimmering blue, one shade lighter than the sky. Other times, it's gray-green, all churned up, with whitecaps and heavy surf. But the best part of the ocean is the air. It has a salty tinge to it. It feels as if you can't breathe it in enough. As if you're flushing your whole system with that oxygen-rich air."

"What does it feel like to have the sea mist on your face?"

"Not unlike spitting rain."

A satisfied look covered Zach's face, a matter decided. "I'm going. Today. I'm headed to the ocean. I'm done here."

Sol answered C.J.'s questions about Danny's habits and favorite places to go as patiently as he could, but he knew that time was passing. He tried to be calm, for Mattie's sake, but he was starting to worry himself. Mattie was right—something felt ominous. That sweet blue sky didn't fool him—he knew a brewing storm was due in. He knew how fickle weather could be.

Mattie was barely holding herself in one piece. He could feel her worry vibrate through the air. Finally, he held up a hand. "C.J., I know you mean well, but time's a-wasting. I need to just go on out and start looking for my boy."

"Look here, Sol," C.J. began slowly, the steadiness of his voice some kind of anchor. "You're right that time is of the essence. But we're not wasting time right now. We need to go about looking for him in a logical way. Do you have a map of the area?"

Sol realized C.J. was being deliberately calm, deliberately soothing, and it felt condescending.

"Sol! Answer him!" Mattie said firmly.

Sol frowned. "No map. Never needed one."

"Then can you draw one for me?" C.J. asked. "Pretend

you're a bird in the sky, looking down at your farm. I want to divide it into grids." He scanned the kitchen counters and Mattie quickly went to a desk and pulled out a paper and pen for Sol. "Give me an idea of how long it would take to get from the house to the edge of the property. Take into consideration the snow."

Sol leaned over the kitchen table and started to sketch out the farm, the fields, the hillsides that surrounded the level land, and the ridges beyond that. He paused for a moment. Where could his boy be? Danny did wander off without telling them what he had planned. Sol hadn't even told Mattie half the times Danny had wandered off. But why now, through this heavy snow? It just didn't make sense. He was half furious with his son for causing his mother such worry, half terrified that something had happened to him.

"Finish, Sol," Mattie urged.

"Mattie, while Sol is drawing the map, describe to me what Danny was wearing."

"He had on a black coat, a black felt hat, a gray sweater," she said.

"How warm were those things?" C.J. asked.

Sol saw panic rise in Mattie's eyes. "What do you mean?" she asked. "Are you worried he'll get frostbite?"

C.J.'s voice stayed low and steady. "I just wondered what he had on his hands. If he had a scarf on. Anything colorful, something easy to spot."

She closed her eyes tightly. "Red mittens."

"Red. That's good!" C.J. said. "That color is easy to spot. What else? Anything missing on the coat rack?"

Mattie walked over to it and looked through some of the coats. She looked over at Sol. "He's wearing his boots."

"That's good too," C.J. said. "They're bigger than shoes

and they're sturdy. His tracks will be easier to follow. No chance of confusing boot tracks with animal tracks, in this deep snow."

Mattie's hands flew to her heart. "Animals! I didn't even think of that. There's a wounded bobcat prowling around the area." Her calm broken, she began to tremble.

"Now, Mattie," Sol said. "Bobcats don't go after people."

She spun toward him, her face contorting with anger. "Don't 'now Mattie' me! You know how dangerous an injured animal can be!"

Sol blew out a puff of air. Mattie's maternal instincts whistled like a tea kettle. He looked at C.J. "She's right."

———————————❦———————————

When Jaime looked up at Zach, something had changed. He looked . . . weird. Nervous. He bounced on the balls of his feet and rubbed his hands together. Then he reached out and picked up Jaime's hand and kissed her palm.

"You could come with me. To the ocean! Right now. Today! Let's take your sports car and head straight to the beautiful Jersey shore!"

Jaime barely resisted laughing out loud at this ridiculous teenager and his silly fantasies but knew she would hurt him deeply if she laughed. She gently reclaimed her hand and worked to keep her face solemn. "Leaving is a big deal to your people, isn't it?"

Zach shoved his hands in his pockets. "I don't have much of a choice, do I? First my father told me to leave. Now Sol."

"From the way I see it, it's all about choices. Your choices. You want it all. You want your family but you want to keep your car." She tilted her head. "Would you actually leave your family? The place you belong? You'd throw it all away because of . . . *a car?*"

"Yes! No! It's not . . . that simple." Gone was Zach's usual peppermint breeze of self-confidence. Suddenly, he looked like a child.

Jaime's voice softened. "But it is, Zach. What you have here—a family that cares about you—most people would give anything to have what you have. And you're tossing it away like it's worthless. You can't have it both ways. You have to make some choices."

His mouth twitched, and for a moment she could see him struggling within himself, trying to fight off the bitterness and resentment. "My father is the one who thinks I'm worthless! He's the one who tossed me away!" His words grew louder and louder until he was shouting at her.

At first, Jaime felt bewildered by Zach's strong reaction, as if she had struck a match and tossed it onto gasoline. She resisted the urge to back away from the blast of his anger. In the barn this morning, Zach had seemed so together for a boy his age, so mature and wise, but now she saw him for what he was: a hurt and lost child, desperately seeking his father's attention. As he ran out of words, his eyes filled with boyish disappointment.

What was worse, she felt as if she were listening to herself. She saw herself in him!

Dear Lord, she sounded like she was seventeen again, as childish as Zach. She may be going about it in a different way, but she was doing everything she could to win her father's approval and attention.

She took a step closer to him. "Zach, I understand."

"No! I don't think you do."

"Listen to me. Tell me if this is what it feels like to you. It feels like having a space, you see, right here—" she tapped her breastbone—"and that space needs to be filled." She let out a deep sigh. She didn't want to chase her father's love anymore. She didn't want to pursue a futile dream. *Just admit it, Jaime!* It was time to call an end to her lifelong quest to be her father's daughter. It was as if someone was rapping the gavel. *Time to move on!*

She looked down at her shoes in the snow. Her feet were getting cold. Maybe her father loved her in his own peculiar way—but it wasn't the comforting kind of dad love she wanted. A love that didn't have any strings attached to it. A love she didn't have to work so hard to deserve.

You want something from your father that he can't give you. No one can. Only God gives perfect love.

Jaime's chin lifted. "What did you say?"

Zach turned to face her. "I didn't say anything."

She looked around her. "Did you hear something? A voice?"

Zach's forehead wrinkled. "Uh, no."

She heard it again. *You want something from your father that he can't give you. No one can. Only God gives perfect love.* She could hear it as plain as day. Where had that voice come from?

A thought came to Jaime then—a thought so luminous it made her feel flushed. It made her heart move in her chest as though it were trying to escape. Something clicked inside of her. Or unclicked.

She needed to talk to someone about The Voice. She needed to think long and hard about it, to examine it and ponder it.

But there wasn't time! Zach stood in front of her, strawberry haired, ruddy faced, handsome, sad. She felt drawn to Zach— she felt *paired* with him—they were so similar. She couldn't wait; she had to tell him what The Voice said. Part of it anyway.

"That dream—of getting your father's love—it isn't going to come true. Not today, maybe not ever. Sometimes, we want more from people than they can give us. They simply don't have it to give."

It made so much sense! But she didn't add what The Voice said about God's perfect love. *That* . . . she did not understand.

Zach was listening so earnestly, concentrating so carefully on what she said, that she wanted to throw her arms around him and give him a big smacker right on his cute little mouth. But she knew he would misinterpret that so she leaned over and kissed him on the cheek. The lightest kiss.

"Thank you," she said.

"You're welcome," he said. "For what?"

"For the offer to go with you today. For everything." Jaime took the keys out of her pocket and handed them to him. "If you want to leave, go ahead and take my car. But only to meet up with your friends. Take them for a ride. Not to the ocean, mind you! You know that Friendly's Ice Cream Parlour at the edge of town, right before the highway entrance? Leave the car in the parking lot, put the keys under the mat."

He couldn't have looked more surprised if she had handed him an airplane ticket to the moon.

She walked past him and stopped. "Just know that you will never find anything out there"—she pointed to the road—"that comes close to what you're giving up here." She swung her arm to point to the farmhouse, like a weathervane turning in the wind. She started up the hill toward the house.

"Wait a minute!" Zach caught up to her. "Where are you going? I thought you needed to be someplace."

"I do," she said. She pointed to the kitchen. "In there."

Zach had never imagined himself behind the wheel of a car like this. Old beaters, yes, like the one he had hidden away on a seldom-considered corner of Sol and Mattie's wooded property. He bought the 1983 yellow Toyota Corolla from a man as old as Noah, and this guy wheezed when he talked, the way Zach imagined Noah might wheeze after climbing a deck or two on the Ark. He paid the old guy $500 plus cleaned out his garage. The car didn't even run, but Zach fixed it up by buying used parts from a dealer. The car had no turn signals, and even in December when it was ten below zero, he had to crank down his window and stick his arm out so that oncoming traffic would know he was turning. There was something wrong with the ignition—sometimes it started, sometimes it didn't. Many a time he had to run alongside that car to get it started, and Susie Blank—bless her—was right there with him, running, pushing, hopping into the passenger side.

It wasn't much of a car and it smelled like a polecat had expired in the trunk, but at least it got him places faster than a buggy. And it gave him time alone for . . . well, time alone with Susie Blank. At least, it *could* provide a little privacy and transportation until his little cousin got into it. When he went to check on it, he had to shovel snow out of it because Danny left the windows open. And then when he tried to turn the key to get the engine started, the key snapped off in his hand. Frozen solid.

As a kid, Zach used to love winter. Sledding, skating, bonfires, snowball fights.

Now? He hated snow. Hated it! It was nothing but a nuisance.

A loud, rumbling noise startled him and pulled his thoughts back to the present. He watched the snowplow head down the road. The driver tipped his head at Zach as he went past, and even turned the plow forward so it wouldn't leave a drift in front of the car. Zach was sure he detected a hint of admiration in the man's eyes. He probably thought Zach owned this car. Such an assumption made Zach grin from ear to ear.

He thought he might drive by Susie Blank's farmhouse and see if she happened to be outside now that the storm had passed by. He wondered if she was still mad at him. He had climbed up on the Blanks' roof last weekend, to rap on Susie's window, like they had planned. She was going to sneak out with him for a midnight drive. He had no trouble climbing up the rose trellis onto the porch. He had no trouble finding a window. Unfortunately, he rapped on the wrong window, and next thing he knew, the sash slid up with a loud screech and Zach was suddenly nose to nose with someone who had salt-and-pepper bushy hair and a weak chin.

"Why, Susie!" Zach said, blinking his eyes in surprise. "You've gone and gotten ugly on me!"

The bushy hair and weak chin belonged to Susie's father.

Susie was no longer allowed to run around with Zach. The next day, after a singing, she told Zach he was an idiot.

"I told you which window to go to!" she told him with eyes narrowed. "I even drew a picture for you!"

"I lost the drawing!" he tried to object.

"Du ware gsoffe!" *You were drunk!*

That, he couldn't deny. And it was at that moment that she called him a Dummkopp! *An idiot!* "My father thinks you will always be a reckless fool. In your heart and in your head. I'm starting to think he's right!"

Whatever happened to mercy? To Christian grace? What

about love covering up all sins and not being steamed at a fellow forever, and forgiving that same fellow for a few measly trespasses? *What about that, Susie Blank? Huh?* But he didn't say it out loud. Even he wasn't that big a fool.

She ended up going home from the singing in Raymond Troyer's buggy, a pimply faced boy who would never risk the wrath of Susie's father.

Maybe Susie was right. Maybe he would always be a reckless fool. He himself couldn't grasp what it was inside of him, where it came from, this terrible urge that drove him to have things he shouldn't have, to want things he shouldn't want. Like this longing to sit behind the driver's wheel in such a car as this red convertible.

Ah, well, why worry about that little spat with Susie on a day like today? He fiddled with a few buttons and switches on the dashboard. The windshield wipers worked like a charm, and suddenly, he had a clear view of the open road.

What if he just took it for a quick spin? Just down to Susie Blank's house and back. It was the chance of a lifetime, the chance for pure happiness. He knew he was standing on a precipice here, that he should think this over very carefully, very thoroughly. Should he drive off in this wonder car? No, never.

But he might.

C.J. picked up the map Sol had left on the table and mentally split it into sections. "Show me the most likely areas that Danny would head to."

"I doubt he'd be in the fields. He must be heading uphill." Sol pointed to the ridge behind the farm.

"Okay, then we're going to take this grid first." C.J. circled that area.

"Let's go," Sol said.

As he started for the door, C.J. stopped him. "Sol, bear with my questions for a few more minutes. Help me reconstruct the last time we saw Danny. Do you remember anything he said? Whom he spoke to last?"

Sol shook his head. "I left him with you when I took Dixie into the barn. What did he say to you?"

C.J. scratched his head. "He wanted Tucker to go with him someplace. He said . . . he said, 'I know what could help.'" C.J. saw Jaime slip behind the men into the kitchen. He tried not to look as shocked as he felt to see her. He assumed she had left.

Jaime looked around the kitchen. "Where's my camera?" She looked at C.J. "Maybe Danny took it."

"Danny would never just take your camera," Mattie said. "Besides, he doesn't even know how to use it."

Jaime winced. "He does," she said. "I showed him. This morning, in the barn. He took some pictures of the baby lamb."

"What would he be trying to photograph?" C.J. asked. "What would 'make it better'?" He looked at Jaime. "He was talking about you. He wanted to find something to make you feel better after you talked to your father." He walked up to her. "Think, Jaime. Did you have any conversation with him that could be a clue?"

Jaime looked baffled. "We talked about all kinds of things. Danny talked . . . a lot." She frowned, then her eyes lit up. "He showed me his box of arrowheads and tomahawks. Indian artifacts. He said that the amazing thing is when you find an arrowhead, the last person who had touched it was possibly an Indian."

C.J. turned to Sol. "Any idea where he would go to find arrowheads?"

Sol grabbed his hat. "There are a few places that we've found them." He pointed to a top section of the map. "It's this northern area."

C.J. held up the map and pointed to sections. "We'll split into three. Cover more territory." He looked around the room. "Where's Zach?"

"Um," Jaime said, "he had something he had to do."

"Is he coming back?" C.J. asked.

Sol narrowed his eyes. "Don't count on him."

Something was going on with Zach that seemed to involve Jaime and Sol, but C.J. didn't have time to wonder what. There was so much drama going on in this little farmhouse! He turned to Sol. "Never mind. We'll split the farm into two, with four quarter sections. Remember to call out Tucker's name too, as well as Danny's. Whistle for him, call his name, then listen for a bark. Call, then listen. Call, then listen. It's important to be quiet long enough to be able to hear a response. The snow muffles sounds." He held the map out to Sol. "If you feel confident that you've searched an area completely, then take this next quarter section. I'll take the lower areas and go north." He glanced at his wristwatch. "We'll meet back at the house in two hours. No matter what. Meet me back here at four thirty."

"What do you mean, no matter what?" Mattie asked. "What then?"

He turned to Mattie. He saw the dread in her eyes. "We'll need to regroup and cover another area. But chances are we'll find him long before then."

Mattie grabbed a coat. "I'm coming with you."

"No, Mattie," C.J. said, his voice kind and indulgent. "It's important that someone remains here. If Danny comes home on his own, he needs to find someone here waiting for him. Otherwise, he'll just go out again."

She stopped putting on her coat. "Bring my boy back. Please." Her mouth was a line.

"That dog won't leave him alone, Mattie," C.J. said. "Tucker is the best chance Danny has to stay warm and get back to you before the storm hits."

Sol and C.J. moved toward the door. Jaime stopped C.J. on the porch. "Do you want me to come too?"

He didn't look at her. "I thought you had a plane to catch."

"No, I don't," she said. "I'm not leaving, C.J. I'll go searching with you."

Sol interrupted. "Stay with Mattie. Keep her mind from worrying."

Mattie joined them on the porch. "What if Danny is truly lost? It can happen to the best of woodsmen, you said. You said it just this morning when you were talking to Danny about your work. You said that even experienced woodsmen get disoriented."

"I also told Danny other things about Search and Rescue—about how to survive in the woods if you get lost," C.J. said. "Remember? Hug-a-tree. Sit-and-stay. He heard those things just this morning."

"It's true, Mattie," Sol said. "God was watching over him, even then."

"Mattie, it's not time to worry yet," C.J. said. "He hasn't been gone that long."

"How often have you found children alive?" Mattie's voice was eerily calm. She was looking deep into C.J.'s eyes.

He tried to think of something to say to her, something that was truthful, and hopeful, and positive. "All the time,

Mattie. Clever kids—ones like Danny—are smart and resourceful."

But Mattie kept looking at him, as if she was reading his thoughts. She had that way about her, of reading a person's soul. Then she pressed her eyes closed for a long second, like she was praying.

For C.J., the silence that followed was studded with guilt. He couldn't tell her about the twins who died last fall, who might have been saved if he had been better skilled at his job. He couldn't tell her the truth, that he felt a spike of worry himself. He had expected Danny and Tucker to have come flying through the kitchen door while he and Sol were dividing up the farm to search for them.

Jaime stepped between them. "C.J. is good at what he does, Mattie. The best, best, best. He's had dozens of successful searches. He doesn't give up."

Relief crossed Mattie's face like a ray of light.

Jaime put her arm around Mattie. "We need to let these guys get started."

As she steered her inside, into the warmth of the kitchen, she looked over her shoulder at C.J. She mouthed the words, "Go find him."

It was all Mattie could do to keep herself from running after the men. How was it possible that Danny would be out in that dangerous and unpredictable world? She stood for several minutes, staring out after them. She pressed her hand flat against the window and shook her head to clear it. Outside, there were now more clouds than sky.

She stepped onto the porch, where she lifted her face to

the sky. Where was Danny? she wondered, sudden tears in her eyes. Where could he be?

Jaime brought out her coat and wrapped it around Mattie's shoulders. "C.J. will find him, Mattie."

Mattie was almost shivering with frantic energy. She was holding herself together with a thin layer of skin and teeth-gritting determination. She had to think about something else, or she'd simply explode. "Where's Zach? You said he had something he had to do. Where did he go?"

As she saw Jaime's hesitation, she was suddenly furious. Why were people keeping things from her? Why did everyone assume she would shatter like a teacup at the first sign of trouble? She wasn't made of spun sugar. "Tell me what you know." She stopped, interrupted by the sudden tightness in her throat.

Jaime's gaze shifted down the driveway. Mattie hadn't noticed before, but that car of hers was gone. "When is he coming back?"

Jaime's eyes darted nervously. "Let's go inside and get warm."

They sat at the kitchen table and Jaime told her what she did know—that Sol had asked Zach to leave, and that Zach had taken her car to meet some friends. Mattie tried not to show it but she was livid with Sol. How dare he do such a thing without talking to her first! It troubled her to see how rigid and unbending Sol could be with Zach. She never imagined Sol would become this kind of man, but he was acting more like Zach's own father every day. Stiff and rule-bound. And she knew it was because Sol didn't want Danny exposed to Zach's errant ways. Sol accused her of babying their son—well, he was trying to create a cocoon of his own making for their boy.

She felt so badly for Zach—she was sure he must have left their home hurt, feeling abandoned. And because of Sol's ridiculous declaration, they had one less person on the farm to help look for Danny.

Mattie rubbed her forehead. How had this happened? She wanted to start this day all over again, to rewrite the way this day had gone. One moment they were all safe, the next moment not.

Mattie blamed herself for Danny's disappearance. She had not been watching him. She had been absorbed in her own thoughts, her own sadness. She had been sleeping . . . while her son wandered into danger. She felt preoccupied, muddled, distracted. She put her hand to her forehead. It was hot and damp, like she had a fever. The tears started up again, out of her control.

Jaime reached out and covered her hand with hers. "It's okay, Mattie," she said soothingly.

But, of course, it wasn't okay.

A cloud smothered the sun, and the kitchen darkened.

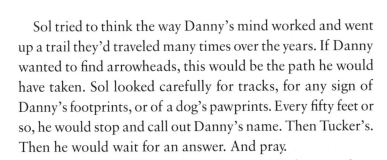

Sol tried to think the way Danny's mind worked and went up a trail they'd traveled many times over the years. If Danny wanted to find arrowheads, this would be the path he would have taken. Sol looked carefully for tracks, for any sign of Danny's footprints, or of a dog's pawprints. Every fifty feet or so, he would stop and call out Danny's name. Then Tucker's. Then he would wait for an answer. And pray.

It was not reasonable, at this point, to panic, because there might be a simple answer to his boy's whereabouts. Since Danny learned to walk, he had been one to wander. He would get absorbed in following something—a bird, a squirrel, and he would follow its trail. Sol used to say he wanted to put a cowbell around that boy just to know where he had gone to.

He passed a place where he and Mattie and Danny had once had a picnic, when Danny was just a toddler. Mattie had led them off the main path and through the trees, following a creek, until they emerged in a sunstruck place she remembered for its wild blackberries. Wind moved lightly in the long grass and the dark green leaves of the blackberry canes shimmered against the earth. The air was full of sweetness and the hum of insects. It was a perfect summer day.

They had spread out their picnic: sandwiches and lemonade and homemade cookies and clusters of Concord grapes from their garden. Sol sat down on the blanket and held Danny in his lap, holding his hands—those plump, dimpled hands—to keep him from pulling off his knitted socks. He remembered thinking idly of his own father's hands, stocky and strong, with skilled, blunt fingers that covered Sol's hands as he taught him to heft an ax or milk the cow or pound a nail. Was that how Danny would remember Sol's hands?

Danny was never one to sit still for long. He succeeded in pulling off one sock, then dropped it and crawled off toward the grassy world beyond the blanket. Even then, he was intent on exploring the world.

Sol watched him pick up a rock and put it in his mouth, a look of surprise flashing across his small face at the strange texture and taste.

"Awful, isn't it?" he said softly, wiping dirt and drool from Danny's chin.

Mattie moved beside him, quietly, efficiently, taking out things from the basket.

"Should he have that in his mouth?" Mattie asked, settling

down beside him, so close he was aware of her sweet scent, filling the air.

"Probably not," he said, unclenching the rock from Danny's fist and replacing it with a torn off piece of bread instead.

They ate lazily, then picked ripe blackberries for dessert, sun-washed and tender. Danny ate them by fistfuls, juice running down his cheeks onto his bib. He lifted a chubby arm to point to two golden eagles, circling in the deep blue sky. Later, when he fell asleep, Mattie moved him on a blanket in the shade.

"This is nice," Mattie observed, settling against Sol, who leaned with his back against a tree. "We should do this more often."

Sol looked at Danny, sleeping so deeply with his head turned to the side, his long hair curling against his damp neck. He kissed the top of his wife's head, warmed by the sun. It *was* nice. It was more than nice. It was a hint of heaven. Mattie looked up at him, expecting him to say something, but he kept his face turned away; he didn't want her to see him so stirred by emotion.

No sooner did the memory of that perfect day seep into his head than it began to snow. Great wet clots of flakes as big as fists. He looked back over his shoulder, blinking hard to get the ice crystals off his lashes. He snapped his head around and peered through the lace curtain of falling snow ahead of him. It was a silent cold, like having your ears stuffed with cotton. The snow and the still, heavy air muffled all sound, except occasionally the sound of a raven calling out as it flew overhead, although he couldn't see it.

He pulled out his pocket watch. Nearly two o'clock. He planned to give this clock to Danny on his sixteenth birthday, the age when his father had given it to him. Sol had never begged anything of God before, but he was begging now. He was, in his heart at least, on his knees with his hands clasped in an agony of pleading. *Please God,* he prayed over and over, like a litany, with every step up the hill. *Please help me find my son. Please keep Danny safe. Please, please, please.*

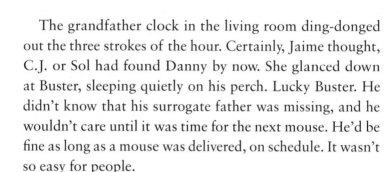

The grandfather clock in the living room ding-donged out the three strokes of the hour. Certainly, Jaime thought, C.J. or Sol had found Danny by now. She glanced down at Buster, sleeping quietly on his perch. Lucky Buster. He didn't know that his surrogate father was missing, and he wouldn't care until it was time for the next mouse. He'd be fine as long as a mouse was delivered, on schedule. It wasn't so easy for people.

She tried to think of ways to get Mattie's mind off the search for Danny and on to other things. She asked Mattie if she wanted to quilt. No. Would she teach her how to bake bread? Seemed as if Amish housewives were always baking bread. But Mattie said no and went into the living room to look out the windows. Jaime decided to try to get Mattie to eat or drink something. She opened the cupboard and found a half-used jar of instant coffee. It was the kind her mother used to make every morning. Jaime unscrewed the cap and inhaled deeply. She suddenly felt overcome with a wave of grief. It really was the little things, like instant coffee, that made Jaime miss her mother the most.

Jaime took out two mugs and reached for the hot water kettle that sat on top of the woodstove so the steam would humidify the room. In the silence that was not quite silence— the sink faucet dripping, the grandfather clock ticking softly, the wind whistling through the trees—her thoughts traveled to memories of her mother.

She stirred in two heaping teaspoons into the mugs, watching the brown crystals dissolve. The smell of the coffee faded, much the way her mother's vivid, everyday presence in her mind was fading. She couldn't remember the whole of her anymore, only bits and pieces: the way she would slip off her shoes as soon as she walked into anyone's home, even if she had a hole in her sock. Or the way her face would light up when Jaime and C.J. stopped by for a visit. Her mother adored C.J. "He's a keeper, that one," she liked to say. Jaime felt so concerned about Danny that her worry over her marriage receded into the background, but it did not disappear.

What kind of card would her mother send her now, if she knew how thin was the string that was holding her and C.J. together? Jaime could imagine it: a big dog like Tucker on the front of the card, and inside it would read "DOG! Depend On God!"

Jaime's hair fell over her cheek as she bent to put a cup of coffee next to Mattie. She settled onto the couch, tucking her legs beneath her. Mattie had her Bible open on her lap and her head was bent over it. Jaime could see the white part of Mattie's scalp where her hair was parted.

Jaime picked up her spoon and stirred the milk into the coffee. *Ching!*

Mattie flinched, as if she hadn't realized Jaime was there.

"Does it help? Reading from the Bible?" she asked Mattie.

Gently, as if it were something very precious, Mattie closed the Bible. "It helps tremendously." She noticed the coffee and reached over to pick it up. "Don't you find that Scripture helps you in times of need?"

Jaime shrugged. "I don't read the Bible. C.J. does, now

and then. Over the last six months or so, he's been going to church." Eve's church. Eve had the gall to invite him to join her one Sunday and he went. Happily. "I guess you could say he's got more of a religious bent than I do. Since my mother died, God and I parted ways."

Mattie looked at her, confused. "What does that mean, exactly?"

"C.J. is just more open than I am to the idea of believing in things you can't see. I tend to accept only things I can see." Or hear? Like, The Voice?

She thought about bringing up The Voice—especially because Mattie seemed to be a little less distracted with worry about Danny. Jaime still wasn't sure how or why The Voice had suddenly bounced into her head. Could it have been that God put it there? And if so, did that mean she was . . . praying? Had Jaime turned into a praying person? Did that mean she would have to start going to church? She wouldn't! She was still mad at God.

The last time she set foot in a church was on the afternoon of her mother's funeral. As she followed the casket out of the church, she left the church behind. The church where her mother had died.

Last June, on a typical Sunday morning, Connie Mac-Comber walked out of church and crossed the street to reach her parked car. She was coming over to Jaime and C.J.'s for brunch. It was their weekly get-together and C.J. always came up with a complicated new recipe to try that required every dish in the kitchen. That morning he was whipping up Belgian waffles with blueberries and pecans. Jaime vividly remembered every detail of that morning. The phone rang, and C.J. reached for it, still whisking egg whites for the waffle batter, the receiver tucked under his chin. As he listened, he stopped stirring the eggs and got a strange look on his face. It was so quiet she heard a wasp buzzing against the window screen. C.J. hung up and came over to sit with her at the table.

"That was the police," he said, in a voice that didn't sound like his. Tight, clogged with tears. "Your mother was hit by a car." He took a deep breath as if he was struggling for air. "The officer said . . . he said . . . she was killed instantly."

Ever since, Jaime felt as if her life was divided into two halves. Before that phone call. And after.

Connie MacComber, a woman who had survived all kinds of hard things—who was deserted by her husband, who had raised a child all on her own—her life was over in a matter of seconds. Killed. Boom, just like that.

The drunk driver who hit Connie MacComber was eventually sent to jail, but that didn't matter to Jaime. It didn't change the fact that her mother was dead. Better to watch your parent die of cancer, Jaime felt, than to have it happen without any warning. So sudden, so premature. Her mother was only forty-nine years old. No time for goodbyes. No time for one last "I love you." So unfair!

How could there possibly be a loving God who would allow a good person like her mother to die in such a needless, senseless way? Jaime concluded there were only two options: either there was no God—and that option didn't work because she knew there were too many mysteries in the universe to think it was all by chance—or, God didn't care.

Now *that* made sense to her. So that's what she settled on. The clockmaker theory. God set things into motion and let things go. Off to meddle in another galaxy!

She knew her mother would object to her theology. She often cobbled together imaginary conversations with her mother: "Listen here, Jaime. Don't go blaming that accident on God. He wasn't behind the wheel of that other car. All things happen for a reason."

But Jaime was never satisfied with pat answers. Her mother used to say that she was forever picking at the Bible and questioning it.

"I'm just trying to understand," Jaime would tell her.

"What's there to understand?" her mother replied confidently. "God said it. I believe it. End of story."

And then Jaime would roll her eyes and call her mother a happy, sappy Christian. She used to make fun of her for believing God spoke to her.

Until thirty minutes ago, when something—Someone?—spoke to Jaime. Today of all days!

A blast of wind hit the house and made the windows rattle, jolting Jaime out of her theological muse. She looked over at Mattie, surprised to see her leaning forward on the couch, peering intently at her. Clearly, Mattie wanted to continue this conversation.

"So, then, for example, you don't believe in the wind?" Mattie asked.

"I believe in the wind. You can feel it and sense it and observe its effects."

"But you can't touch it or see it." She picked up a book on the coffee table and dropped it on the floor with a *thunk*. "Gravity is all around us, from the heavens to the ground under us." She plucked a feather from a couch pillow and raised her arm as high as she could, then released the feather. She watched it flutter to the ground. "Isn't *that* believing in something you can't see?"

One thing that always nagged at Jaime about such declarations of belief: wasn't there such a thing as just having faith in faith? "Believing in a law of nature like gravity isn't really the same as believing in a God who is involved in our everyday life." She might have sounded a little more defensive than she intended.

Mattie looked out the window and released a sigh. "To me, it is. Powerful, invisible, majestic, mysterious. And faithful. Gravity is a force utterly consistent in its steadiness on all items—great and small. God is faithful even when we are not."

For a moment, Jaime forgot that she was in an Amish farmhouse on Christmas Eve, that the hosts' child had disappeared, that her plans for Christmas had fallen apart. For a moment, she was having a debate about the existence of God, just like she used to with her mother. She felt like a teenager again, trying to figure things out for the first time.

"Oh Mattie, do you honestly believe that God who created the universe and put laws of gravity into place—do you honestly believe he cares about our little, tiny planet in this small Milky Way galaxy, among billions of galaxies! Do you really think we're of any significance to him? And you really, truly believe that God actually cares about your thoughts and your choices and your concerns?"

Mattie locked on to her eyes. "I do." She leaned forward on the couch. "I believe God reveals his loving nature in all kinds of wondrous ways. Every single day. From sunrises and sunsets, to the families he's given to us to share this life, to—" Buster gave a loud squawk from his box in the kitchen and Mattie smiled—"to birds and animals. To the greatest miracle of all—the birth of the Christ child, a holy God entering into his creation to redeem it. God's perfect love is all around us, Jaime. But if you shut your eyes to all the light he has given to you, you can't see the evidence of his love."

God's perfect love? There it was again! What did that

mean?! Okay. *Fine!* If Mattie wanted to push her on this topic, Jaime was going to push right back. "Mattie, if you believe that God is really out there, truly watching over everyone, that he's a good and loving God like the Bible says . . . then why are you so anxious about everything? Why do you seem to live as if you're expecting a catastrophe at every turn? So if you pray, why worry? And if you worry, why pray?"

Mattie looked at her for a long while with an inscrutable expression on her face. Quietly, she stood and left the room.

Jaime heard Mattie's bedroom door shut gently but firmly. *Bad, bad idea.*

In the silence that remained, all Jaime could hear was the ticking of the old clock and Buster in his box, hissing and spitting like he was angry.

Why does my mouth seem to run ahead of my brain? She had said all the wrong things. She had only made things worse for Mattie. She was trying to distract her from worry, only to bring it right up again. She rubbed her face and leaned her head back against the couch.

She let out a loud sigh. She had blown her chance to ask Mattie about The Voice.

Not long after C.J. set out, there came the first shrieking, biting gust of wind. It sent the falling flakes spinning and whirling crazily and whipped at the loose snow on the ground. The knife slash of the wind cut through his clothes and felt as if it were shredding his lungs. He glanced at his wristwatch: twenty minutes after three. He pulled his collar up around his neck and pushed on.

C.J. had encouraged Sol to head up to the ridge that lined

the farm's property, hoping he would be able to catch sight of Danny and Tucker from a high vantage point. He wanted to stay on the low ground—to follow the stream that fed the pond. All kinds of streams crisscrossed these Amish farms, carving crevices through pastures, and he knew those banks were extremely unstable. He carefully followed the stream, calling for Tucker and Danny, listening for a response, scanning the area for signs of a boy and a dog. The stream was smothered under a blanket of fresh snow, the willows that lined the banks were all fringed with it. He tried to look as far as he could see for any sign of movement, but the whole world looked frozen dead.

He was trying not to panic. As an experienced SAR volunteer, he knew of countless stories just like this—a family was enjoying themselves, got busy and distracted, a child wandered off—and the day ended in tragedy.

But not today. Not this Christmas Eve. He wouldn't let a tragedy happen again, not like it did last summer. He had to be able to find Danny. Even without Tucker and his nose, C.J. had enough experience now to find Danny. Didn't he?

Enough. Funny how that word seemed to keep hitting him in the face lately.

His mind drifted to Jaime's comment last night, that sometimes love just wasn't enough. A few weeks ago they'd had a terrible argument. It was a Sunday morning and he had planned to meet Eve for church. He asked her if she wanted to come along—like he always did—and Jaime acted as if he had insulted her. "Why should I come?" she said. "I would just get in the way."

"What's that supposed to mean?" he had said.

"What do you think it means?" she asked.

"Jaime, what's going on? Why are you overreacting?"

"You don't love me," she said. "You've never loved me."

"I do love you." He tried to keep his voice steady. He could see she was steaming like a tea kettle and he wasn't sure why.

"Not enough! You don't love me enough."

"I do love you enough," he said. But it worried him that it would never be enough.

Before he could say anything more, she darted into the bedroom, slamming the door behind her and locking it.

C.J. knocked on the door. "Jaime? Please open up. Jaime, I don't know what's made you so upset."

He heard nothing from the other side of the door but her muffled crying. Even with his best intentions, the best he could give, he'd somehow failed. He had listened for a minute, and then he picked up his car keys and left to meet Eve.

How could he love Jaime enough when she always wanted more?

A blast of cold wind slapped him in the face. The wind shifted from southwest to due west and the sky was low and gunmetal gray. Something caught his eye in the open field he was walking through—an area of discoloration against the snow. He picked up his pace until he reached it. It was discolored, all right—a stain of fresh blood on the snow. C.J. sank down on his knees in the snow and searched around to see if he could find any clues—any fur or tracks or indication of what this was. Fresh kill? He leaned forward to examine the blood and caught sight of something slightly buried—a stick? A rope? Carefully he dug it out. His heart started thumping wildly. It was a dog collar. A small tuft of yellow fur was still attached from where the collar had been torn off. Bitten off.

C.J. had found Tucker's collar.

He cupped his hands around his mouth and called out,

"Danny! Tucker!" Then he listened for a response. Nothing. He called again and again. Nothing.

He glanced at his wristwatch: ten minutes to four. He *had* to keep going.

When Jaime's cell phone started to vibrate, she dove for it and moved into the farthest reaches of the living room before she answered. Mattie was still upstairs and she wasn't sure if she was mad at her or not. The last thing she needed was to add to Mattie's aggravation by having a cell phone in the house.

"Hello?" she answered in a whisper.

"Jaime! This is Marilyn. Marilyn Steffey. From Sears Portrait Studio. Listen, I spoke to my boss who spoke to her boss who spoke to the store manager, and we're willing to offer you a promotion if you'll come back. You can be the studio manager."

"But . . . *you're* the studio manager," Jaime whispered.

"I've been promoted too! I'm going to be the district manager."

"Oh," Jaime whispered.

"Aren't you thrilled? This is highly unusual in a dismal economy. You should be thrilled!"

"I am. So, so thrilled," Jaime whispered.

"Then why don't you sound thrilled? It's a boost in salary, Jaime, from being an associate. You're on a *career* track."

"Sorry. Laryngitis," Jaime fibbed. "Could I call you back? On Monday?"

Marilyn was disappointed. "I suppose."

"I'll talk to you Monday. Merry Christmas, Marilyn. And

thank you." Jaime hung up. So, she had her job back. She leaned back and rested her head on the top of the couch, staring at the ceiling.

The grandfather clock eked out another hour. This announcement was mercifully short: three o'clock. When Mattie heard it, she knew she should get downstairs in case the men came back soon. She wiped away her tears, splashed cold water on her face, and smoothed her hair. Down in the kitchen, she was pulled to the window, as if Sol and C.J. might already be turning into the yard with Danny. A layer of ice coated the glass.

Jaime joined her by the window. "Maybe we should go feed the animals. So when the men come back with Danny, they don't have to go back out."

Mattie nodded, grateful for something to do. Grateful for Jaime's brave optimism. They put on their coats and Jaime wrapped up Mattie's face with a scarf as if she was the mother and Mattie was the child. Jaime walked ahead of Mattie, shielding her from the wind the way Sol would do. In the last twenty-four hours, she and Jaime had switched roles. Jaime was the strong one now. Mattie was the weak one.

Mattie had lived in Stoney Ridge all her life, but she hadn't known it could snow this hard or be this cold. It seemed the wind blew the stinging, biting flakes right through her, as if she were invisible. The horses stood in their stalls, hunched and sad against the wind that slashed through the cracks in the barn walls. Mattie's hands were as clumsy as clubs, her arms and legs stiff, as she pitched hay to the horses and broke the ice in their water buckets. But every time she drew a breath of the icy air, it felt as if a knife were sliding into her chest. She was *that* cold, inside a barn. What was this wind doing to a small boy in a thin coat?

Mattie was measuring out grain for the horses when Jaime came into the feed room.

"I'm sorry, Mattie. I didn't mean to offend you earlier. I feel terrible that something I said made you cry."

Mattie was genuinely surprised by that comment. She finished filling the bucket, closed the wooden lid, clipped it to keep out mice, and sat down on it, facing Jaime. "You didn't offend me. Just the opposite. You were right. I went up to my room and asked the Lord to forgive me for being so fearful. For ever doubting him."

It was more than just that. Back in her room, as Mattie prayed, confessing everything to God, withholding nothing, telling him all of the thoughts—even the ugliest ones that kept swimming through her head—something broke inside of her. She felt peace within her swell and grow, connecting her back to the world. She grew calm, became again that wide tranquil river, accepting the world and carrying it easily on her currents. Danny belonged to God, not to her. If she truly believed that, why was she living as if she could control all the circumstances that surrounded him? She couldn't. She never could. She exhaled a stream of breath she had been unconsciously holding on to . . . for how long now? Four years? Five? She felt lighter. She felt centered. She felt like her best self.

The mystery of prayer! The ability to commune with the Lord God! It never ceased to astound Mattie that God would want to know her every thought. To think she had tried to hide her dark thoughts from God, to stuff them down, to pretend they didn't exist. It shamed her to think she could. She had never considered herself to be an overly prideful person, but pride was sneaky; it had so many twists and variations to tangle a person. Listening to Jaime talk about her mother's death, seeing the anger she harbored toward God for not preventing it—why, Mattie recognized herself in Jaime! She was angry with God for denying her a child. She assumed God had turned his face from her—without cause or explanation. Without love.

She remembered a sermon her grandfather Caleb Zook had given once from the book of Job, how he pointed out that Job and his friends assumed the trials of his life meant he had lost favor with God.

"Not true!" her grandfather had said. "God's favor doesn't suddenly disappear. He is kind and trustworthy from generation to generation. But our faith in God should never be fastened to circumstances. God promises to never leave us, nor forsake us—*whatever* our circumstances."

That reminder was just what she needed this very afternoon. She hadn't lost God's favor. He had never abandoned her. He was right in the midst of their lives—of Danny's disappearance, of her grieving over her miscarriage, of her barrenness. He was there yesterday, today, and tomorrow—with all its unknowns. *Emmanuel. God is with us.*

Jaime's head was down. She slowly lifted her eyes to meet Mattie's. "What if Danny isn't found soon?" she whispered. "What then?"

Mattie's breath caught. *Not found?* Jaime had voiced aloud a fear that had nagged at Mattie all through the long afternoon.

Jaime went over to sit next to her. "Bad things happen. Even to good people like you and Sol."

"Bad things do happen, but not randomly. Not without purpose."

Holding her elbows, Jaime leaned forward. "But they do, Mattie. My mother was walking across the street after leaving church and she was killed by a drunk driver! You can't tell me *that's* not random and purposeless!"

"That accident passed through the hands of God. Good hands. It wasn't random and it wasn't purposeless. It was your mother's time."

Jaime stood up and walked a few paces. "What kind of God is that? This world is so dangerous! So unpredictable! If he can't—or won't— protect people who love him . . . what's the point of having faith in him? What kind of perfect love is that?"

"God never promised us a life without pain or suffering, Jaime. He's promised to never leave us in the midst of that pain. He promised to bring purpose out of that pain. Emmanuel, God is with us. That was the name given to Jesus. Emmanuel." She patted the feed bin so that Jaime would sit down again. "*That's* perfect love, Jaime. God will never leave you nor forsake you. Not on earth. Not in heaven."

Jaime sat down next to Mattie and leaned her elbows on her knees, rubbing her forehead as if she had a headache.

Maybe she does have an aching head, Mattie thought. *She's been trying to make sense of her mother's death without any help at all from God. That would give anyone a headache.* She rubbed Jaime's back in a soothing, circling motion.

How strange, Mattie thought. Minutes ago, she was thinking that Jaime was the strong one. Now they had flip-flopped again. She was feeling brave. It felt so good! She hadn't felt brave in a very, very long time.

Mattie let out the breath she had been holding. She looked around the barn, satisfied that everything was taken care of. She picked up the bucket of grain with her clumsy, mittened hand. What had she forgotten? The laundry. She needed to get started on the laundry. If she missed a day of laundry, it spiraled out of control.

Zach thought he might love this car. The word *car* seemed too humble, too ordinary, for this engineering marvel. It should be called . . . The Dream Machine. Sleek, curvy, red like a race car, a V-6 engine with 220 horses under the hood. The thought of all that power in his hands astounded him.

When Jaime first offered to let him take the car, he sat in it for the longest while before he turned on the ignition. He figured she was just kidding, or would change her mind. But as he watched her in the rearview mirror as she walked up to the farmhouse, she never looked back. When she stepped inside the kitchen, he turned the key. The engine sprang to life. The dashboard was lit up with red numbers and symbols like the instrument panel of an airplane he'd seen in a magazine. Even after this car had spent a night partially submerged in the pond! Thankfully, it was the back end that was submerged. Zach stepped on the gas a few times and revved the engine, to make sure the exhaust pipe spewed out any leftover pond water. He fiddled with the radio and switched stations fifteen times—ah, to finally be in control of something. *Anything!*

He flipped a few more switches. All of a sudden, he heard some strange noises. The black roof started to lift! Zach panicked and flipped more switches. Too late! The top was folding up like an accordion. He whipped his head around to see if Jaime had seen the top go up. No sign of her. He shifted the car into first gear and inched toward the street. Then, he turned left onto the road. Slowly at first, as if he were driving something made of delicate bone china. As his confidence grew, he pressed the pedal a little harder. No one was on the freshly plowed roads. He pressed another button and suddenly felt his chair grow warm. Seat warmers! What more could a man ask for in life, than a red sports car with seat warmers? *Just one more thing.* A woman like Jaime Fitzpatrick sitting in the passenger seat.

Still, for Zach, today would always be his best day. Life just could not get any better than this! He was driving a convertible—fire engine red!—and he had just been kissed by a beautiful English woman—practically on the lips. He relived the kiss for a moment. It was, quite possibly, the most exquisite kiss he had ever been given. Apologies to Susie Blank, the only other person he had kissed—and Susie was a first-rate kisser. But this Jaime Fitzpatrick! It was like your first cup of Starbucks coffee when all you'd ever tasted was Folgers. Not that he was much of a coffee drinker, but he did take Susie to Starbucks once in his Toyota Corolla, just to see what everybody was talking about. Then he went home and tried Mattie's coffee. No comparison. *None!*

If only that kiss with Jaime had lasted longer than two seconds. What could it have meant? Was it possible she was attracted to him? Was it her way of letting him know she was interested? That she might be available? Okay, this was bad—a bad thought, a bad series of thoughts, a bad, bad path he was going down. Unspeakably bad.

For over an hour, he'd driven the car slowly up and down every plowed road he could find, not straying too far from the house. Snow was starting to pile up on the seat next to him. He scooped up handfuls of it and tossed it over the side before it melted on Jaime's leather upholstery. He pressed the button to close the top, admiring the convenience of this mechanical task. He couldn't wait to show the car off to his friends—and yet . . . he was in no hurry to find them. He felt a prick of conscience, like a small pebble in his shoe that he could ignore if he wiggled his toes. Maybe he should turn this car around, go back to Sol and Mattie's, find Jaime, and try to act like a normal person. Set things straight.

He definitely should turn back. It was time he grew up. Turning around would be the wise, mature thing to do. The right thing to do. It would be the first step in the long direction of mending his ways.

But before Zach was quite ready for that, he pressed on the gas just a little more, then a little more. Something caught his eye out the window—a golden eagle soaring in the sky. He wondered if he could clock how fast that eagle was flying. The long stretch of road ahead looked clear, with just a dusting of snow. He pressed on the pedal a little harder. 25 miles per hour. 35 miles per hour. 45. Amazing! This was as fast as his 1983 Toyota Corolla could ever go—that old beater started to shake at 44 miles per hour as if it might splay apart.

As Zach zipped along at speeds he'd never traveled—faster than the snow dropping from the sky—his thoughts were filled with the wonders of the automobile. 50 miles per hour. 55, 60. Had any invention changed the world more than the car? The miracle of modern machinery! 70 miles per hour, 80. The car was driving as smooth as velvet. *Astonishing!*

Up ahead, he saw a bend in the road. He pushed on the brakes, tightening his grip around the leather steering wheel to anticipate the turn. He was halfway around the bend when suddenly, inexplicably, illogically, he knew where Danny might be.

He pushed harder on the brakes to turn around. Instead, the car started to slide toward the snowbank.

Down in the basement of the farmhouse, Jaime helped Mattie wash the clothes in the washing machine. It was such a simple machine—an agitator fed by gasoline. It got the job done nicely. She thought of the washing machine she had picked out from Sears last year—all kinds of bells and whistles. Literally. The sounds drove her crazy. Dozens of choices—wash with warm, rinse with cold, hot with hot, cold with cold. Were her clothes any cleaner than Mattie's? She doubted it.

Mattie and Jaime hung the clothes on the indoor line that Sol had rigged up, quiet for a few minutes, their elbows occasionally knocking together as they worked, until Mattie said out of the blue, "What's on your mind?"

The sadness Jaime had been trying so hard to suppress oozed to the surface. "I envy you."

"Me? Whatever for?"

Where to begin? After Mattie had come back downstairs, Jaime could see she had been crying. Her eyes were swollen, her skin was blotchy. But she radiated a calmness that was almost palpable. "So many things, Mattie. For your home, your family, your faith."

"You can have all of those things. You *have* all those things."

Jaime shook her head. "My father says that nearly every marriage is tainted in some way. Either one or both parties settled, or someone is dissatisfied, or someone is cheating or at least considering it. And he should know. He's been married a number of times."

Mattie rolled her eyes. "Rubbish."

"It's true! Maybe not for you and Sol, but for the rest of us."

"You and C.J. have a good marriage."

Jaime shook her head. "He's involved with another woman."

Mattie lifted her eyebrows in disbelief.

"A woman he works with. Eve. They have a connection that we just don't have anymore. I can tell. He's slipped away from me." She bit her lip, and her eyes stung. "Everyone I've loved has disappointed me. My father never even wanted a child—that's why he left my mother. I was six months old and he walked out the door. Then my mother died! And now C.J. is giving up." She bit her lip to hold back tears that stung her eyes.

Mattie didn't say a word. Her face didn't change expression in the slightest way. She finished hanging a small blue shirt that must have belonged to Danny, and let her hand graze it gently. She put the bucket that held the clothespins back on the shelf, then went upstairs to the warm kitchen.

Didn't she hear me? Jaime thought as she trotted behind Mattie. *I just spilled my deepest, most gut-wrenching secret, and she acted like it was no big deal!* Like she knew it all along! It suddenly occurred to Jaime . . . maybe she had already known. Had C.J. told her, this very morning?

Mattie took out a large bowl and placed it on the counter. Then she gathered flour, Crisco, salt, and measuring cups. Business as usual.

"Mattie? Don't you have anything to say?"

Mattie poured a cup of flour she had measured into the bowl. She turned to face Jaime. "I see your husband's determination to find my son. He's not going to give up. I doubt he would give up on his marriage either." She went back to measuring out more cups of flour. "But you. You seem to give up pretty easily. Just because life can be hard, it doesn't mean you give up. Maybe you've been influenced by the way your father gives up on things. Like your marriage—you're

168

giving up on that without a fight." Mattie spoke slowly, out of the beautiful calm she seemed to wear like a coat. "Maybe you've even given up on God."

Jaime sat at the table, watching Mattie fold the Crisco and flour together with a large fork. She moved with lightning speed, yet she never hurried. It amazed Jaime. Coming from anyone else, Mattie's pointed comments would have sounded like an admonishment, a scolding, but from Mattie, it just sounded like the truth, gently spoken. Was it the truth? About Mattie's insight to C.J.'s nature, Jaime had to agree. She'd never seen him give up on anything.

"What about Eve?"

"Have you ever asked him about Eve?" Mattie stopped folding the ingredients and looked at Jaime. "Have you ever talked to him about all that worries you? Really talked?"

Jaime closed her eyes. No. She had been too afraid of the answer.

Was Mattie right? *Do I give up too easily? Even worse . . . am I like my father?* She covered her face with her hands. She was. She was just like him! Starting things and never finishing them. Jobs. School. People. Jumping from one thing to the next. She folded her arms on the table and clunked her head on it.

Mattie put her fork down and sat at the table next to Jaime. "Jesus told a story about a good shepherd who had ninety-nine sheep in his fold, but one was missing. He left everything to go look for that one lost sheep." She paused to let it sink in. "What if you're that lost sheep, Jaime? What if God brought you here this weekend, and let your precious car slide into the pond, and permitted a snowstorm to change your plans? All of your plans! And what if Danny's disappearance is part of God's plan to bring you into his fold?"

She placed a hand on Jaime's arm. "And what if God brought you to me this weekend to help remind me that the Bible is true? That God's Word will stand forever."

Jaime lifted her head. She hated to ask this question, but she had to. "Even . . . if things don't work out the way you hope they will?"

"You mean, if Danny isn't found?"

Jaime gave a quick nod.

Mattie squeezed her eyes shut. "I will deal with that if and when I have to. For now, I have a pie crust to finish." Then she rose to her full five-foot self. "Two kinds of pies, I think I'll make. Apple and pumpkin."

Jaime lifted her palms. "Why pie?"

Mattie looked at her as if it was the most obvious thing in the world. "Because pie is Danny's favorite dessert."

The clock struck the hour, the quarter hour, the half hour.

Just then, Sol burst through the kitchen door. "Is he here?" His eyes met Mattie's and his face fell.

Not a minute later, C.J. arrived. He looked at Sol and shook his head. "Did you see any sign of him?"

"No," Sol said. "No sign at all."

Mattie opened up the stove to let the two men warm their hands. She took their scarves and gloves and laid them on top of the stove to dry them. The two men stood in front of the stove, faces red and wind chapped, rubbing their hands in a heavy silence.

Jaime mixed up some cups of instant coffee and handed each man a mug. She wished the pies were ready for them, but Mattie had just slipped them into the oven.

C.J. took a sip of coffee, then turned to Sol. "Show me the map you made. Show me what area you've searched."

Sol spread the map on the kitchen table. He pointed to the areas he had covered.

As the two men worked up another plan, Jaime could sense the change. This was getting serious. It was like a bad dream. Danny had been gone over three hours now. The chance of hypothermia was real.

Sol's voice stayed low and calm, like C.J.'s. Mattie—she was silent. She made some sandwiches for the men and wrapped them carefully in wax paper to be taken out on the next search. What was going through her mind? Jaime had no idea.

Jaime thought this was probably the most frightening thing that had ever happened to Mattie and Sol. They weren't used to accidents, to bad luck, to tragedy. They hadn't lived with it, maybe, the way she had.

C.J. put on his scarf and his gloves to prepare to go out again. As Sol stood to join him, C.J. shook his head. "No, Sol. You're not going out this time."

"Why not?" Sol asked.

"Yes, why not?" Mattie echoed.

C.J. exchanged a glance with Jaime. She would know exactly why not and he was hoping she wouldn't say.

This was standard operating procedure. If there was reasonable chance of a Deceased Find, family members must not be there. *Must not.* A parent's reaction at discovering his child was deceased could create yet another dangerous situation. The worst story C.J. had ever heard had happened to Tom Flint, one of his SAR buddies. A sixteen-year-old boy had gone missing during a river rafting trip. The father insisted on joining the search. The father found his son first, drowned, caught between rocks. The father panicked and jumped into the water to get his son. The father drowned too. Then Tom nearly drowned, trying to retrieve both bodies.

Mattie and Sol were waiting for C.J. to answer them. Right now, with the storm kicking up and the temperature dropping like it was, the chance of finding Danny alive was growing dim. How could C.J. tell them that? The thought was hideous to him.

"I'll go with you," Jaime said. "You shouldn't be alone out there."

"He won't be," Sol said. "I'm going with him."

C.J. cleared his throat. "I'm sorry, Sol. Not this time."

Sol took a few steps up to C.J. "Why not?" He grabbed C.J.'s jacket lapels. "Why not? What do you know that you're not telling me?" His voice was barely a whisper.

"I don't know anything." C.J. spoke calmly and slowly. Inside, though, he felt his heart going crazy. He had to get hold of himself; he did search and rescues like this all the time. But he didn't know the victims, not like he knew Danny. He had seen anguish on parents' faces before, he empathized, but he hadn't felt the anguish, not like this.

"Then why don't you want me going with you?" Sol asked, eyes narrowed. "I will not trust my son's welfare . . . to an outsider!"

"Sol!" Mattie was horrified. "This man"—she pointed to C.J. and her voice quivered—"this man is doing everything he can do *for* our son's welfare!"

C.J. looked at Mattie. The look in her eyes shook him to the core. So trusting, so hopeful. An idea took shape. "Sol, I think it's best if you can get to a neighbor's farm and see if you can collect some men to join in the search."

Sol brightened. He loosened his hold on C.J.'s coat lapels. "We should have thought of that sooner."

C.J. turned to Jaime. "Can you call the sheriff's department to let them know we need help?"

Jaime reached into her pocket and pulled out her cellphone. "Voilà!"

Sol looked at her hopefully.

She dialed 911, listened, squinted at the face of the phone, dialed again. Then she snapped it shut. "Dead battery," she said in a flat voice.

C.J. turned back to Sol. "Have someone contact the sheriff when you round up everyone. They need to bring lanterns and flashlights and dogs. I'll be back at this house in one hour. Meet me here and we'll send out people, two at a time."

"C.J. is trained at this," Jaime told Sol. "Listen to him. He will find Danny."

C.J. looked over at her. He was grateful she didn't promise he would find Danny alive. Where could that boy be? Where was Tucker? Had they been hurt? Why couldn't he find any trace of them other than that collar?

Jaime threw two large sandwiches into a brown bag she found tucked in a kitchen cupboard. She poured the rest of the coffee into a thermos, closed the lid tight, and packed it all in a sack for C.J. She handed him the sack just as he was heading out the door. She grabbed her coat and followed him out on the porch. He stood for a moment, looking out at the falling snow, at the wind that blew it every which way. Too soon, it

173

would be dark. She knew that could be disastrous for Danny and Tucker. Between the trees across the street, she could see where the sun lay low in the sky, hidden behind gray clouds.

"C.J., what do you know that you're not telling them?"

He shifted his gaze down toward the pond. "Something had dragged off a fresh kill. I followed it as far as I could, but then I lost the tracks."

"What kind of tracks?" She put a hand on his arm. "It could have been a fox catching a rabbit. Or a squirrel. It might have been nothing at all."

He gave a slight shake of his head. He reached into his pocket and pulled out Tucker's collar. "Bobcat tracks."

Tears sprang to Jaime's eyes. This wasn't the way things were supposed to go. Danny should be home by now! Tucker should be staring at her with those mournful brown eyes, hungry for his dinner. "Any other clues? Fabric or . . . dog hair?"

"A few tufts of Tucker's fur. There was some kind of a tussle. If Tucker saw the bobcat going after a rabbit, I wouldn't put it past him to get in the middle of it."

Even Jaime knew that all the training in the world couldn't change an animal's natural instincts. Not Tucker's, and certainly not the bobcat's. Bobcats were solitary animals, unlikely to go after a large animal—or a little boy—but if it felt threatened . . .

"C.J.," she said softly, "what if—?"

He turned to her and put a hand in the air to stop her from saying it. "Keep Mattie's mind on other things than that." His face was pale, still, but determined. He gave her a weak smile.

"I have been." Jaime tried to find a smile of her own, but she was too ill at ease. No, *scared* was the word. She was plain scared.

He took her hand, raised it to his lips, and kissed it. She felt the press of his lips on her knuckles and his breath warm on her skin. Then he gave her Tucker's collar and vanished into the snow.

She thought about The Voice. If that was God, and if he had decided to start up a conversation, maybe she should respond. Isn't that what prayer was supposed to be? She looked up at the sky. *Are you listening, God? Do you really care? If you do, please, please, please bring that boy home safely.* She put the collar into her coat pocket so Mattie and Sol wouldn't see. *And Tucker too. I'll never ask you for anything else. But please bring them home safely.*

Jaime stood on the porch for a moment, watching the sky, until she was so cold she couldn't stand it any longer. She turned and caught sight of Sol and Mattie through the kitchen window. Jaime watched Sol move toward Mattie as if pulled by gravity. Mattie's face lifted at the sight of him. He cupped her face lightly in his hands as they kissed, and then she raised her hand and their palms touched briefly, lightly, a gesture so intimate that Jaime looked away.

It was, quite possibly, the most heartbreaking embrace she had ever seen.

Although it seemed C. J. had been walking for a long time in a perpetual dusk, he sensed the hour was truly getting late. When night fell, it would be as dark as a cave and the chances of finding Danny and Tucker would grow even slimmer. He fought down swells of panic. Where could they be?

He was about to cut through a field when he heard a shout from the road. C.J. turned and saw a figure waving at him.

The man started running toward C.J. He stopped when he was fifteen feet away.

The man cupped his hands around his mouth and yelled, "Did you find Danny?"

Zach! It was *Zach!*

C.J. shook his head.

Zach waved his arm like a windmill. "Follow me! I think I know where he is!" He turned and ran back down to the road.

C.J. followed close behind, picking up speed. Zach hopped a fence and started running up the road. Puzzle pieces that were floating through C.J.'s mind started to find a place. If Danny had gone down along the road, that would explain why they couldn't find any tracks. The horses, the cars, the snowplow would have erased any sign of a small boy and a dog.

Zach didn't quit running. They'd gone half a mile up the road when he finally cut off and vaulted over another fence with easy grace. He stopped to wait for C.J. "We could keep on the road, but it'll be faster if we cut through this field. Can you keep up?"

Could he keep up? What did this kid think, that he was an old geezer? Of course he could keep up! He gave Zach the thumbs-up and climbed over the fence—he had to take it in stages and hurried to keep up with him. Zach acted like an Indian scout following a faint trail. He seemed to know exactly where he was heading. There wasn't as much snow on the ground under the thick canopy of the trees, but other than that, the conditions weren't much more favorable. The wind still had a way of hitting them hard in the face.

They came to an open field—the same field where C.J. had found Tucker's collar. Zach crossed the field, passing the traces of blood without even noticing them. As C.J. ran past the spot, he saw that the wind had covered the mess with fresh snow. If he didn't recognize the stubby cornfield, he wouldn't even be able to find that spot. Not without Tucker's nose. The wind struck in volleys, driving the corn-hard pellets of snow into his face. He stumbled, went sprawling, and got mired up to his knees in a fresh drift. Scythes of snow slashed at his eyes. He slogged on, trying to keep up with Zach.

Zach kept up a brisk pace across the field. It was the same direction C.J. had been going until he lost the trail. Through another canopy of trees, they came to a bridge. Past that was an old cobhouse. Zach stopped.

"That's it," Zach said. "I bet my life on it. They're in there."

He pointed to the back of the cobhouse, to a large object partially covered in snow. It was growing dark, but even C.J. had no doubt what it was—Zach's hidden car.

"Danny!" C.J. yelled. "Tucker!"

Zach started down the hill, but C.J. grabbed Zach and made him stop for a second, to listen for a response. Any sound.

Silence.

"Danny! Tucker!" he cried, and his voice echoed in the darkness.

A sound then, faint.

C.J. and Zach started to run down the hill toward the car. "Danny! Tucker!"

C.J. heard a muffled sound.

"Woof!" It came again. "Woof! Woof!"

Relief flooded C.J., replacing the fear that had shadowed him all afternoon. He and Zach pushed through the brushy copse and broke at last into the clearing.

"Danny! Tucker!"

They bolted toward the car, jumping through thick drifts.

Tucker's large head appeared up on the dashboard. "Woof!"

C.J. reached the car first and pulled open the door. Tucker leaped out, practically tackling him. Zach pulled the back door open and reached in headfirst to find his cousin. Danny was curled into a ball in the corner of the backseat. He didn't speak. His eyes flickered open and shut. His face was pale and his lips were blue—signs of hypothermia. But he was found. And he was alive!

"We have to get out of here, pal," Zach gently told him. "We have to get you home."

Mattie peered out the window, but she only saw darkness and the reflection of the kitchen's lamp. Winter always had an ability to make a body feel insignificant before the awesome forces of nature. It had been dark a good half hour when she heard a strange noise. With the wind blowing hard enough to peel the bark off trees, Mattie thought it had peeled something loose off the house. Then the wind stilled a moment, as it did sometimes, as if sucking in its breath to blow even harder, and she heard it again. It was a definite human sound, floating up from the driveway. Was she imagining it?

No—Jaime heard it too.

They exchanged a look and froze where they were, craning to hear it. A great whoop split the air like the clang of a fire bell, followed by a brief, sharp noise.

Jaime jumped out of her seat. "It's Tucker! That's his bark!" She ran to the kitchen door and opened it wide. "Mattie! They're back! They've got Danny!"

Lumbering up the driveway were two large figures, one of them holding a child in his arms. Tucker was running up and back, barking with excitement. Mattie ran down the porch steps and flew down the driveway, not even caring that it was snowing and bitter cold and that she didn't have a coat on.

As soon as she reached them, C.J. held Danny out to her. "He's okay, Mattie!"

She held her son close to her chest, feeling his small body against hers. He was as light as a feather to her as she ran with him back to the house. Once inside, she rushed to a chair near the woodstove, just like she had with Zach—was it only twenty-four hours ago? It felt like a lifetime.

She was barely aware of Jaime tenderly untying Danny's shoes, pulling off his socks, his gloves, looking over his hands and feet for any signs of frostbite. C.J. had filled up some bowls of tepid water for Danny's hands and feet.

"We need to warm him up slowly," he said, hovering over Danny. He kept checking Danny's eyes for dilation, he explained to Mattie. "He's getting his color back. He did a smart thing, getting in that car. It kept him and Tucker out of the wind."

"Why did he go to the car?" Jaime asked.

Zach crouched beside Danny. "My guess is because it's close to the eagles' nest. That's how he discovered my car in the first place—he was poking around there just last week, spying on the eagles."

C.J. slapped his forehead with the palm of his hand. "That's what he meant by saying he thought he could help. He was going to take a picture of the eagles." He looked at Jaime. "He wanted to make you feel better after that call from your father."

"The camera," Danny squeaked out in a raspy voice.

Everyone stopped what they were doing and looked at him. Danny gave a slight shrug to his shoulders. "I saw the bobcat go after a cottontail and Tucker started barking." He stopped to swallow, as if it hurt his throat to talk.

Mattie stroked his hair. He was so cold! But his cheeks had lost that ghostly white look and his lips were pinking up.

"Tucker went after the bobcat and they got into a fight, so I ran to the car."

"You did the right thing, Danny," C.J. said. "You did just what Tucker wanted you to do. He was trying to protect you."

"Then Tucker jumped on the car and I let him in," Danny said slowly. "But I lost the camera."

Slowly, C.J. placed Danny's bare feet into the bowls of tepid water. "You did a smart thing. You kept yourself safe and Tucker safe. Probably kept each other warm."

Danny closed his eyes, then opened them wide. "Buster!" he squeaked out. "He needs a mouse! For dinner!"

Mattie was laughing, then crying. Danny was home and he was unharmed and everything was going to be all right.

Moments later, Sol burst through the kitchen door. Behind him was a covey of Amish men and boys, peering into the kitchen. Zach's father, Eli, pushed his way through the group to get in the kitchen. Sol stopped abruptly at the sight of Mattie crying, holding Danny in her arms by the stove.

"Is he . . . ?" Sol asked.

Danny turned his face toward his father and reached out a hand.

Mattie nodded, too moved, too relieved, to speak. She still didn't trust her voice to speak.

"Er ist okay?" Sol said. "Dank der Herr!" *He is safe? Thank God!* His eyes filled with tears. He crouched down beside Danny and stroked his head. Tears fell down his cheeks and he didn't even wipe them away.

He stood to face C.J. He grasped C.J.'s hand with both

of his and shook it. "Thank you, C.J. Thank you for finding my boy."

"Don't thank me," C.J. said. He pointed to Zach. "It was Zach. He figured out where Danny had gone."

Sol walked straight to Zach and grabbed him in a powerful, wordless hug.

Later that night, after dinner, Mattie tucked Danny into bed while Sol and Zach went out to the barn to check on the livestock. C.J. and Jaime made noises about leaving, but Sol wouldn't let them. The storm was still raging, and besides, he told them, "We need to celebrate Christmas together! The best Christmas of all!" Mattie was so pleased when they agreed to stay.

She would never forget this weekend—a weekend of miracles. Danny was unharmed, protected by Zach's car despite three hours in freezing temperatures. An hour after getting inside and getting warmed up, Danny was hungry and worried about Tucker's cuts from the run-in with the bobcat. C.J. assured him Tucker was fine, that an injured, three-legged bobcat was probably in much worse shape than a big, strong dog. And that started Danny's litany of questions about dogs. Mattie smiled, still unable to say much, her heart was so full of gratitude.

Danny nearly fell asleep during dessert, and she quietly steered him upstairs for a warm bath before bed. She sat on the edge of his bed as his eyelids grew heavy in the middle of a story he was telling her about the day's adventure. She kissed him gently and tucked him in, running her hand over his soft hair. He was so big.

She closed her eyes. *Oh, Lord God,* she prayed. *Thank you for blessing me with the gift of my son. Thank you for blessing me with life and love and laughter.*

Stairs creaked, then floorboards. Her heart quickened at Sol's footsteps on the stairs, and then he stood in the doorway, his face flushed from being outside. She reached her arms out to him and he reached for her. When she kissed him, his lips were cool against her own.

* * *

After a long hot bath, Jaime wrapped herself in a towel. It felt scratchy and stiff, dried days ago in the winter sun. She heard a knock on the door and C.J.'s voice on the other side. "Mattie wanted me to bring up some fresh towels."

She opened the door for him and he handed them to her.

"Mind if I brush my teeth while the lantern is here?"

She stepped back so he could get in the bathroom and shut the door behind him. Tucker wanted to come in too, but there wasn't enough room for the three of them. "It is so dark and so cold here. I've never realized how much I take electricity for granted."

C.J. went to the sink and brushed his teeth. "Not just electricity." He spit out a mouthful of toothpaste. "I've noticed a lot of things we've taken for granted."

He shook out the toothbrush and set it in a glass. He turned back to Jaime and cocked his head. A softness came over his face. They were silent for a moment. The faucet dripped, and steam swirled. She heard Tucker's heavy breathing, right up against the door, sounding like a bull in a ring.

"Are Tucker's cuts okay?"

"Yup. Just a few surface scratches. Not really sure if Tucker scared off the bobcat or the bobcat scared off Tucker."

Jaime felt water drip from the tips of her tousled hair strands, tucked in a towel. She turned away from him and studied the nightgown Mattie had loaned her. A rivulet of water ran down the small of her back. He took a step closer and put a hand on her bare shoulder. He kissed the water dry on the back of her neck. His stubble found the curve of her neck, then gentle lips made their way. She was paying him no mind.

"The towels smell like sunshine."

"This skin you're wearing is pretty sweet smelling." He slipped his arms around her waist. "Pretty beautiful too."

"No . . . ," she laughed, embarrassed, and tried to squirm out of his arms and reach for her nightgown. "Don't be silly . . . I'm not beautiful."

Jaime could feel him still, arms around her, tensed, steady.

"When are you ever going to believe me? That I think you're beautiful? That when I tell you I love you, I mean it." He said the words slow and low.

Jaime took a deep breath. She was glad she wasn't facing him. "And Eve? Do you love her too?"

C.J. dropped his arms. "Eve? What about Eve?"

Jaime kept her head tucked down. "Since she started working at the school last fall, she's all you talk about. Every day, you bring her up. Something she said, something she did for you. Baking brownies, taking Tucker for a walk. I know you stay late to talk to her after school. She even called you today! Earlier—right when the car came out of the pond. Remember?"

"I remember." He turned her around to face him. "So . . . you think I'm having an affair with Eve?"

"I don't know. Not yet, maybe, but it's inevitable."

"You are *jealous* of Eve." It wasn't a question. It was a statement.

"No! Of course not. How ridiculous." She sat on the edge of the tub and thought about Mattie's encouragement to be honest with each other. To really talk to each other, about everything. Thoughts, feelings, hopes, and dreams. Even fears. She took a deep breath. "Yes. Yes. I am jealous of Eve. I think she is the kind of woman you should have married. The kind you wish you had married. Someone who doesn't have issues trying to please her father. Someone who isn't a mess. Someone who would be a wonderful mother. Not like me. I'd make a terrible mother. A child would need years of therapy just to survive having me as his mother."

There. She said it all. She could feel C.J. watching her. He sat down on the floor, leaned his back on the tiled wall, his hands resting on his bent knees. "Jaime, look at me."

She lifted her eyes.

"You're right. There is something I haven't told you. It's about Eve."

Here it comes. She knew it. All along, she *knew* it.

"Jaime, Eve is seventy-three years old."

He was smiling his big, wide smile, the one that was so contagious. She looked at him in wonder.

C.J. dropped his chin to his chest, trying hard not to smile, not to laugh, but when he lifted his head and their eyes met, a short laugh rolled out of him, then another, and another, until he was doubled over. She felt so foolish. So foolish and silly. Then the laughter left his face and he stared back at her for the space of three slow, thunderous heartbeats. She was surprised he couldn't hear it, the beating of her heart.

When he saw she wasn't laughing, he stood and held his

hands out to her, pulling her close to him, wrapping her in his arms. "I love you, Jaime. Nothing can change that." He brushed her cheek with the words, with his lips.

She stood on tipped toes, hair still dripping. "Thank you, C.J."

"You mean, for this?" His eyes glinted and he kissed her, and soon they were a laughing mess.

Mattie was right, Jaime thought later, in bed, after C.J. had fallen asleep with his arms wrapped around her. Love was much more than words. It was a phrase her mother would have appreciated and used in a greeting card. Maybe tomorrow she would tell C.J. about The Voice, that she was a praying person now. Tomorrow, for sure. Right after she told him that she had quit her job at Sears Portrait Studio. She knew she couldn't go back to it, even if she was returning to a promotion.

Instead, she had an idea of what she wanted to do with her passion for photography. She wanted to get back outside, where she belonged. To photograph nature and wildlife and—dare she think it?—to become a photographer of the Amish. Not of their faces, of course, but of their lives. To chronicle the day-to-day activities of these simple, peace-loving, yet oh-so-fascinating people, for future generations to know that such a way of life could exist. Quilts hanging on a clothesline on a snowy day, like the photo that had won the *National Geographic* contest. And children at play, and well-tended barns, and buggies traveling down a country lane. Would it work? Would anyone buy her photographs? She took a deep breath. She didn't care. She would be doing something she loved.

Jaime yawned. Tomorrow, she would tell C.J. everything. Mattie was spot-on—she and C.J. needed to talk more to each other, from-the-heart kind of talking. But right now, she felt so cozy, lying here with her back pressed against him. The simple touching of his body to hers. And with her hand still in her husband's, she fell asleep.

Christmas Morning

On Christmas morning, Mattie rose early and made break-fast, decorating the plates of eggs, bacon, and hash browns with sprigs of parsley, grown from a little pot she kept by the sunny kitchen window.

"That sure smells good," Sol said as he came in from the barn, kissing her cheek.

At Danny's place at the table was a pile of gifts covered by a dishtowel. He lifted it and added a new whistle he had carved late last night, sitting by the fire. He looked up at Mattie, suddenly shy.

"Eagle whistle." He shrugged. "To remember." He rubbed his chin. "He could have died."

"But he didn't," Mattie said quietly but firmly.

Sol took something from his pocket and lifted the dishtowel in front of Zach's place.

"What are you up to?" Mattie asked.

Sol got a look on his face like Danny did when she caught him with his hand in the cookie jar. "It's Zach's broke-off key to his car. I got it loose this morning by using a blowtorch."

Mattie raised her eyebrows. "You're encouraging him to keep the car?"

Sol pretended to look indignant. "I'm doing nothing of the sort! I'm just . . . taking the advice of a wise woman I know and letting him chart his own path."

She smiled. "You, Solomon Riehl, are a wonderful man."

Sol's cheeks reddened. "Only because you help me be a better man." He took off his coat and hat and hung them on the wall peg.

"There's something else I need to tell you," she said.

"Sounds serious."

She nodded. "It is." She took two mugs from the cupboard and poured coffee into them. She handed one to Sol and he sat in a chair at the table. She leaned with her back against the kitchen sink. "I'd like to consider fostering children. A baby. A foster baby. I think it would be good for all of us—you, me, and Danny. And it would be good for some child out there too, who needs a home like ours. I'm not giving up—I'm still hoping we'll have another baby. But I have a great longing to be a mother, Sol, and maybe that doesn't mean I have to bear the children. Maybe God has kept me from bearing another child—for now—because he wants me to care for a motherless child. And you—you're such a fine example of a man. You could have such a strong influence for good on a child who doesn't have any men in his life."

There. She said it. She had practiced this speech last night as she was getting ready for bed. She watched him carefully to see his reaction, but he didn't seem at all surprised or resistant.

He took a long sip of coffee. Then another. He looked out the window. "Boy or girl?"

Hope filled her. "Either." She tilted her head. "Does it matter to you?"

He shook his head. "You are what matters to me. You and Danny. If you'd like us to foster a child, then we can do that."

"You mean it? You're not just saying yes because it's Christmas?"

He smiled. "I think it's a fine idea, Mattie."

Mattie put down her coffee cup and crossed the room toward Sol's open arms. She was smiling wide and laughing, really laughing.

The sun came up in a sky that was hazy with frost. The air shimmered so with the cold that it was like looking at the world through a sheet of oiled glass.

After breakfast, Danny opened his gifts and Sol read the Nativity story from the book of Luke—first in German, then in English.

And then the Riehls had church to go to, and it was time for the Fitzpatricks to be on their way. Mattie invited Jaime and C.J. to come too, but when they heard the service would last three hours, that a hymn lasted as long as twenty minutes, and that the entire service was in German . . . they quickly declined.

As Jaime went downstairs, she realized she was leaving this Amish farmhouse as a different person. How could so much happen in less than two days? On Friday night, she arrived here as a complete mess, a nutcase! Her thinking was so scrambled, so mixed up. She had such a warped sense of what love should be. No one would ever be enough to fill that empty space inside—not her father, not her mother. Not even poor, dear C.J. It wasn't a human-sized space. It was too vast, too deep. She wasn't quite sure all that it meant—about God being the only perfect love—but today, Christmas, she was starting to have a glimpse of what it meant. She was loved by a love that was *enough*!

She heard the grandfather clock ding-dong its message: half past seven. She knew they had better hurry to leave so that the Riehls could make it to their church service by eight. And she and C.J. hoped to meet Eve at her church by nine. C.J. wanted Jaime to meet Eve, face-to-face.

In the kitchen, as they said goodbyes, Jaime stooped down to envelop Danny in a bear hug. She even tried to hug Sol, though it ended up being awkward, kind of a half hug. Next Jaime turned to Mattie, taking in her pale hair and clear skin, her gray eyes, calm and penetrating. Jaime's eyes filled with tears and she tried to blink them away. Mattie took her in her arms the way a mother held a child. Jaime felt as if she was being given a hug and a prayer all wrapped up in one. Mattie made her promise to come by for dinner.

"Soon!" Mattie insisted. "I'll get you liking my chow-chow yet."

Jaime wasn't sure about chow-chow, but she knew she'd be back to this little farm. Very soon.

Zach opened the kitchen door. "Ready to go?"

Jaime sniffed and wiped her cheeks with her hands. She followed C.J. outside. In front of the kitchen step was a horse harnessed to a sled. "My car! I completely forgot about it with all the excitement going on last night. Zach, did you leave it at Friendly's Ice Cream Parlour?"

"Well. Not exactly." Zach flashed her one of his incredible smiles. "Kind of a long story. A funny story, actually. I'll tell you all about it as we head into town." He looked back at Mattie and Sol. "I'll be a little late to church. But I will be there. Tell my folks I'll be there."

He took a step toward the sled, then spun around to face Jaime. He patted down his jacket and reached inside his pocket. He pulled something out and held it up. "Hey—I almost forgot about this! After they yanked your car out of the pond, Danny was climbing around inside it when he thought no one was looking." He raised an eyebrow at Danny. "He must have left this in the car." He tossed it to Danny.

Danny caught it, gazed at it for a moment, then tossed it to Jaime, grinning his jack-o'-lantern grin. "You keep it. Dad and I can make another."

It was the owl whistle.

Mattie waved a dishcloth until she couldn't see the three figures on the sled any longer. She smiled, wondering how Jaime was going to take the news that Zach had to abandon her red car in a snowdrift after not quite making a bend in the road. She was glad not to be a witness to that particular conversation.

Sol and Danny disappeared into the barn to get the horse and buggy ready for church. Mattie knew they'd be out in a few moments, eager to leave. She should go inside to finish the dessert she had prepared for church dinner, and put on her bonnet, but not quite yet. She took in the sight of this dazzling Christmas morning, air as cold and clean as mountain ice, of the snowy fields that sparkled like crushed diamonds, of glistening icicles off roof gables, of the winter visitors at the bird feeders she and Danny kept filled with sunflower seeds. She took a deep breath. The air held the distant scent of pine, a clean scent, fresh as the snow.

Emmanuel, God is with us.

The world was immense, unpredictable, and sometimes a frightening place. But right now her son was in the barn, laughing and peppering his father with questions. And Sol was with him, buckling the buggy traces to the horse, patiently answering his son, and she didn't have to cook dinner today.

This was her life. Not quite the one she had imagined as a girl, but it was her life, built with care and attention, and it was good. She felt good.

And God was with them.

She climbed the porch steps, pulled open the kitchen door, and went inside to get ready for church.

Discussion Questions

1. Mattie and Sol's world is very different from the world in which Jaime grew up, and probably the world you grew up in too. What attracts you to the Riehls' world?

2. The Amish do celebrate Christmas, but not the way the English do. For most Amish families, gifts are given only to the children. And a large meal will be shared among extended family. The Amish have a saying: "The best things in life are not things." Does it ever seem as if a typical American Christmas—the commercialization, the excess—has gotten out of control? What are some ways you can tone down your family's traditions so there is more time for true Christmas peace?

3. Mattie's inability to have another child consumed her. She described herself as turning into someone she didn't want to be. At a baby shower for her friend Carrie, she said she felt bitterness as real as bile in her throat. "But why couldn't it be she who had a baby? Why was it that her sisters-in-law and friends could do something that she couldn't seem to do?" How does Mattie's

experience after her miscarriage help you feel compassion for those who struggle with infertility?

4. Mattie and Jaime forged an unlikely friendship. Besides the snowstorm, what circumstances in their lives drew them together?

5. What do you think it says about Jaime that she likes to view the world through the lens of her camera? Did Jaime's insecurities frustrate you? Why? Did you ever see yourself in some of her insecurities? Did your thoughts about Jaime change at all as the story progressed?

6. In many ways, C.J. seems to be an ideal husband. He is considerate and kind. He's even a good cook! How did you feel when C.J. wondered how he could love Jaime enough when she always wanted more? Do you think we expect too much from people?

7. How did you feel about the fact that Jaime often questioned and doubted her relationship with her husband? What was the underlying, unresolved problem for Jaime that she projected onto C.J.?

8. What are your overall thoughts on Jaime's father? Have you ever known anyone like him—big ideas, poor follow-through? Discuss Jaime's revelation that she was expecting something from her father that he simply didn't have to give.

9. What was your response to The Voice? Have you ever sensed God was trying to tell you something? Was it audible? Or was it a knowing, a deep inner prompting?

10. Jaime challenged Mattie by saying that her faith didn't seem very effective in a crisis. "If you worry," she told her, "why pray? And if you pray, why worry?" Have you ever felt that your faith isn't effective? Why are circumstances and feelings the wrong focus of faith? What should be the focus of our faith?

11. In the midst of a crisis, Mattie took some time alone and prayed—*really* prayed. She poured out her soul to God. After that, "she felt peace within her swell and grow, connecting her back to the world." Even though the crisis was not resolved, Mattie was filled with the peace of God that passes all understanding (Phil. 4:7). When have you had a similar experience?

12. The theme of this story is "Emmanuel, God is with us." What does that mean to you? How does the belief that God is in the midst of your life—every up, every down—change your perspective?

Acknowledgments

My first thank-you belongs to the Lord Almighty, who entered into creation at Christmas to bring redemption to a fallen world. That's the message of this little story: Emmanuel—God is with us.

Thank you to Celeste Butrym, of Guide Dogs for the Blind, for explaining the ins and outs of Search and Rescue. Those involved in SAR work are true heroes.

Thank you to my agent, Joyce Hart, of The Hartline Literary Agency, who believed in my writing abilities before I did. To my editor, Andrea Doering, for her insight, intelligence, and patience. And to Barb Barnes, grammar-maestro, who made this a better book all the way around. To the excellent team at Revell (Twila Brothers Bennett, Michele Misiak, Janelle Mahlmann, Jennifer Nutter, Donna Hausler, Deonne Beron, Claudia Marsh, Mary Molegraaf), for their enthusiasm, professionalism, and hard work.

Finally, I'd like to thank the people in my foxhole: Lindsey Ciraulo, Wendy How, Nyna Dolby, and Tad Fisher for the first, crucial read.

And as for my family, what can I say? You supply me with love, support, and *constant* material.

And my love and thanks to all of the readers who've come with me to Stoney Ridge this far.

Suzanne Woods Fisher is the author of *The Choice*, *The Waiting*, and *The Search*—the bestselling Lancaster County Secrets series. Her grandfather was raised in the Old Order German Baptist Brethren Church in Franklin County, Pennsylvania. Her interest in living a simple, faith-filled life began with her Dunkard cousins.

Suzanne is also the author of *Amish Peace: Simple Wisdom for a Complicated World* and *Amish Proverbs: Words of Wisdom from the Simple Life*, both finalists for the ECPA Book of the Year award. She is the host of "Amish Wisdom," a weekly radio program on toginet.com. She lives with her family in the San Francisco Bay Area and raises puppies for Guide Dogs for the Blind. To Suzanne's way of thinking . . . you just can't take life too seriously when a puppy is tearing through your house with someone's underwear in its mouth.

You can find Suzanne online at www.suzannewoodsfisher.com.

Meet Suzanne online at

 Suzanne Woods Fisher   suzannewfisher

www.SuzanneWoodsFisher.com

Don't miss the other novels in the
LANCASTER COUNTY *Secrets* series.

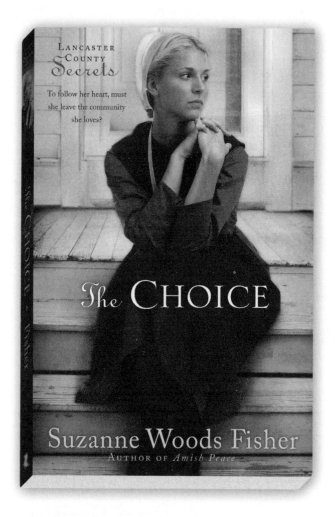

To follow her heart, must she leave
the community she loves?

Sometimes we find love
where we least expect it.

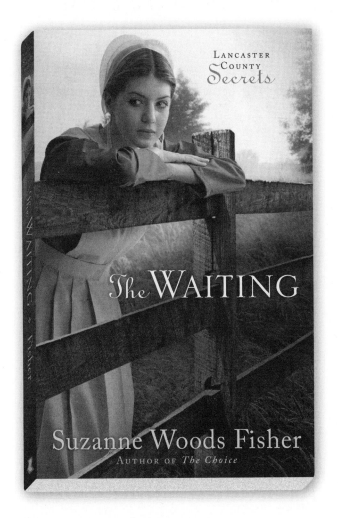

You will find yourself transported into the world of the Amish
and deeply invested in these wonderful characters.

Be transported into the world of
the Amish and the lives of these
wonderful characters.

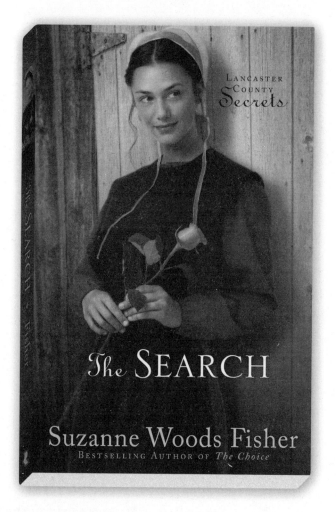

LANCASTER
COUNTY
Secrets

The SEARCH

Suzanne Woods Fisher
BESTSELLING AUTHOR OF *The Choice*

Fifteen years ago, she made a split-second decision.
How could she know that choice would change so many lives?